THE SECOND COMING

ROGUE ACADEMY, BOOK ONE

CARRIE AARONS

This is a work of fiction. Names, characters, businesses, places, events and incidents are either the products of the author's imagination or used in a fictitious manner. Any resemblance to actual persons, living or dead, or actual events is purely coincidental.

Editing done by Proofing Style.

Cover designed by Okay Creations.

Do you want your **FREE** Carrie Aarons eBook?

All you have to do is **sign up for my newsletter**, and you'll immediately receive your free book!

For Mark.

Thank you for answering every single one of my questions about the BPL. Call it payback for all the soccer you talk at me.

1

JUDE

Most football players loathe running up and down the pitch in the pissing rain.

It's bloody wet, usually cold, mud cakes in your boots and you can't see a damn thing. It's hectic, and your senses have to adjust sharply and quickly to make sure you play just as well as when the heavens haven't opened up.

It's chaos. Pure bloody chaos.

I guess it's a good thing I thrive in chaos.

The papers tomorrow, the ones they sprinkle on every tube train and coffee shop counter will say I'm unstoppable. That Jude Davies, the second coming of God when it pertains to English football, is so unbelievably talented, not even Mother Nature and her merry band of hurricane winds and rain can stop him.

They might be right, in some sort of sense. But they don't know the real truth.

That inside, I'm a maniac. A raw beast who gets high off of pandemonium.

My legs barely register the force pummeling through them as I barrel down the field, the grass and mud kicking up behind me. Defender after defender fall away, their mediocre talent no match for me. When I'm focused, when my eyes train on nothing but that woven white net at the other end of the pitch; it would take the world imploding to stop me.

"Pass! Pass it!" The Rogue Football Club's manager, Niles Harrington, screams at me from the sidelines.

Ignoring him, I forge on, my blinders on so I see nothing but the goal and the wanker who's going to try to block my shot in front of me.

A player from the opposing team slides in, mud and water flying everywhere. It's a storm of shit, flying right for my body, and I tighten every muscle from my abs down to take it. Mentally, I deflect the attack, and my body follows suit. My feet spring from the earth, propelling my body up and over where he's just tried to illegally side tackle me. Hopping over him, I get right back in sync with the ball that continues rolling down the field.

And just like that, I'm there, punting the ball woven with a mix of hexagons and pentagons with all my might. The keeper, evil prick, dives left, but I fake him out, a shit-eating grin on my face. My kick aims right, and before I even see the ball cocoon in the back of the net, the crowd lets out a deafening roar.

"YESSSSS!" I shout, throwing my arms up to the god's, challenging them to stop me.

No one will. Because no one will ever understand why I play as hard and as selfish as I do.

My teammates tackle me from behind in celebration, patting me on the head and howling at the victory my game-winning goal, scored in the ninetieth minute, has brought us. *The Beatle's* "Hey Jude" blasts from the stadium speakers, the anthem they play whenever I score a goal.

"You brilliant git!"

"Saving our arses once again!"

"Piss off, Trolls!"

The praise is a mix from my teammates and the crowd, the last sentiment aimed at the other team. My club, Rogue FC, is one of two teams residing in the inner zones of London. The Tartenham Trotters are the other, but our supporters have called them the Trolls, a biting nickname, since before I was born.

From the middle of the pitch, the referee sounds the final whistle, and the game is over. Immediately, happy, drunken fans begin to stream out of the stadiums. Presumably, they'll take their celebrating to the closest pubs and stay there well into the morning hours.

But me? I have a date with three international models, my mates, and a bottle of tequila.

"You're a selfish bugger, you know that?" Niles, our manager, sticks his finger in my face the minute I walk into the locker room.

Rolling my eyes, I harrumph and give him a cheeky grin. "But a brilliant one, right?"

His face, wrinkled and bulging where his eye sockets embed, is so angry, it might catch fire. A few seconds tick by as my teammates mill around me, heading for the showers or packing their bags to go home to family or out to the club, like me.

"Yeah, a fucking brilliant moron," he finally relents, rubbing a fist into my hair in an exasperated, silent praise.

I know Harrington thinks I'm a loose cannon. That's because I am. But I'm the bloody maniac who wins him games, so he can't argue with my tactics. Once he walks off, I quickly shower and change into the black jeans and black T-shirt I brought with me. Looking at them, you'd think they were just plain clothes. But if you were to feel the material or saw the price tag at the time of purchase, most people would call me a damn idiot for paying that much for something to throw on.

Looking at myself in the mirror and running both hands

through my damp, midnight-black hair, I muss it until it looks like I've been balls deep in two birds all day instead of out on the pitch. My skin, the color of milk chocolate swirled with caramel, stretches at the corner of my mouth where a smug grin paints my full, scarlet lips. Thanks to my family's Grecian background, I look like I've been on a yacht in Santorini, and my green eyes sparkle with satisfaction that I'm so damn beautiful.

"Do you think anyone loves Jude more than he loves himself?" Alexander Karlsson, a tall Norseman who plays right winger, smirks at me in the mirror.

"Nah. He'd probably suck himself off if he could manage it." The Rogue defensive back, Luigi Buosco, spits out this dirty comment.

These guys, lifelong Rogue FC players, still poke fun at me because I only played my debut game earlier this year. The youngest guy in the lineup, I went into the Rogue Football Academy at seven years old. I've spent almost my entire life playing the game, living for it, being around players and shooting for a top spot on the only team that matters. Now I'm bouncing back and forth from the premier league to the academy, and I want to stay in London. No bloody way do I want to go back to dorm rooms and settling for second best. I want it all, right now. I may only be twenty, but I'm better than any of the first team players and the best forward this club has ever seen.

Notice how I didn't include a probably in there. Because I am ... the best forward this club has ever seen.

Niles and the rest of the owners of Rogue, though ... they think I'm a hothead. A liability who can't be controlled. They're right. But they're also thick if they think they'll win a trophy without me.

"Well, from what I've heard back from the kit chasers, my dick is bigger than yours," I mouth off, a smug smile directed at both of them.

Alexander laughs it off, while Luigi shuts up. He has a bad habit of sleeping with women who aren't his wife.

"Going to TwoTen tonight, Jude?" Alex asks, pulling on a suit way too fancy for my liking.

I nod, lacing up a pair of black combat boots. "Nowhere else I'd rather spend my time here in London. Except on the field that is."

"I'll see you there. Unless, of course, Harrington sends you back down tonight." His eyes dance with the giddy prospect of my failure.

Not that my teammates don't like me, but in professional sports, everyone is your competition. Even the players you are supposed to work with. Everyone is gunning for everyone else's spot, and you have to be cutthroat as hell to make it.

"Have a good night, mates." Tipping my head, I don't grace Alex with a response about our manager's impending decision.

Walking into the hallway of the stadium, I cherish the moment of silence in one of the hallowed halls. That is, until my best academy mates Kingston Phillips and Vance Morley come stumbling through the player's exit, champagne and sexy women in hand.

"Let's go, Davies!" they shout, having tagged along to London to watch my game, even if they hadn't been called up to play.

But a voice from the other direction catches my attention first.

"Jude, you bloody moron! Why? Why do you do this stupid shite?"

Barry McCathers, my publicist, barges down the hallway, the leggy babes standing just behind me titter with laughter.

His thin frame makes him look like Jack from *A Nightmare Before Christmas*, but the sharp angles of his face are always intimidating. It's how he bullies reporters, brand reps, and the talent alike into doing whatever he says. Well … everyone except for me, that is.

He throws a newspaper at my face, and I'm fully ready to see my name and words like "superstar," "Prince of the Premier League," and "savior" splashed across it.

Except, that's not the story they're choosing to feature on tomorrow's edition. No, it's a full front-page spread, with pictures, about me out at the club last weekend. Smoking a cigarette.

"Who the bloody hell even caught these pictures? I was standing in a back alley!"

Barry pinches the bridge of his nose, trying to keep his temper under control. "Have I not told you a thousand bloody times that anyone, anywhere, can get to you? That even in the sanctity of your own bedroom, they can hack your computer camera to record a video of you singing 'Dancing Queen' in your skivvies."

I cock an eyebrow. "Well, Barry, old pal, now I know what you do on your nights off."

The models waiting in the wings giggle some more, and I hear Luigi, who's come out of the locker room, trying to paw at one. His wife won't be happy about that if she finds out … although he'll probably just buy her another million-pound piece of jewelry to shut her up.

"This isn't a bloody joke, Jude! Niles has already called me, just a minute ago from his car home. He's sending you back down."

Fuck. My blood goes cold, and all the elation I felt from the victory is instantly squashed.

"It was one bloody cigarette! I was drunk!" I plead. "Come on, Barry, you can fix this. Pay someone off."

He shakes his head. "It's already running, Jude. By this time tomorrow, you'll be the laugh and disgrace of every British citizen. The Prince of the Pitch, ruining his goddamn talented lungs because he's too bloody irresponsible to have an ounce of self-control."

I want to slam my fist into the brick wall behind his head. Fury courses through my veins, and when this kind of rage starts to overload my system, I don't retreat. I attack, even harder than I normally do.

With a cocky flick of a smile, I saunter toward my friends and the girls, calling to Barry over my shoulder, "Watch how bloody irresponsible I can be."

2

ARIA

"He's back, again."

Patricia, the head seamstress, walks into the airy building we work in on the outskirts of the Rogue Football Academy grounds.

"Hmm?" I muse idly, trying to sew a seam that just doesn't want to stay straight ... or closed.

The machine jammed this morning and I've had to do everything by hand. But then again, I'd rather use my hands. There is something soothing about making everything with your own ten fingers, instead of relying on machines.

"Jude. He's back again. The first team sent him back down. Apparently, Harrington is furious over the smoking photos." Patricia sits down at her station across the room, checking the lettering on the back of one of the new away kits.

I roll my hazel eyes, feeling the exhaustion already seep into them. Damn it all, I even had two cups of coffee this morning. I guess that's what happens when you only get three hours of sleep a night.

"You love to gossip about him. Me? I don't have time to worry about what a nutter like that is gambling away. If I had the money he did, I'd follow every rule to the letter."

Louisa, the only other woman on the grounds under the age of forty, snorts. "You follow every rule to the letter as it is. Any more and you'd be a nun."

She and Patricia look at each other and laugh.

"Har har, that's fine. Mock me, but I'll be finished with my work long before you today."

"Oh, come off it, Aria. I just think he's dishy." Louisa sighs.

I ignore her, not wanting to get into this conversation for the hundredth time. Patricia would agree, even though she's old enough to be Jude Davies' grandmother, and they'd go on and on about who the best players at the academy are, and what dodginess they were getting into at night.

And like I said, I really don't have time for this. Because unlike Patricia and Louisa, who have worked in the kit and clothing wing of the Rogue Football Academy for almost thirty years combined, I've only been here for six months. In that time, I've taken on not only my position as a junior seamstress but have also talked William, our boss, into letting me take some grounds keeping shifts as well. That means after my six-hour day here, I will be doing laundry, making beds, and tidying up after the spoiled brats in the main dorm houses.

But, I need the money. When it's a life or death situation, it doesn't matter that your hands bleed at the end of the day, or that you only sleep three hours a night.

And ... this was life or death.

After graduating from secondary school on the day of my eighteenth birthday, I ventured out on a mission to find a job. Growing up in Clavering, England, the town that has housed the most elite British football academy, seeking out a position at Rogue was the first thought that jumped into my mind. It's close to home, and with the buckets of money sitting in the owner's bank account, I knew they paid staff well. Both of which I needed ... both of which my family direly needed. When I interviewed with William, I wore my best, albeit a third-generation hand-me-down suit. My long, blond hair was pinned back behind my ears, and I left my face free of makeup. The blokes at school never missed the opportunity to comment on my curves or sharp cheekbones ... or the eyes that flashed like a sphinx's if even the smallest hint of mascara was applied to my lashes. So I went in there looking like a straight-laced, boring goody-two-shoes ... and I got the job.

While the rest of my classmates were deciding which university they'd attend, I never even gave myself the room to dream for it. I knew it would never be an option, no wiggle room about it. So, instead of nurturing that flame of hope, I extinguished it long ago.

Just like I extinguished any thoughts of Jude Davies ... or his band of scoundrels. The boys at Rogue are superstars, the next class of world athlete celebrities. And they knew it. Being the same age as most of the students here only made things worse. Unlike Louisa, who is ten years older but still trying to attract eighteen- to twenty-year-olds at her day job, I try to dress in baggy clothing and keep my hair in a tight bun.

Still, these boys are shameless. Fit, beautiful, gifted, spoiled wankers. If they want something, they take it without asking. A pat on the bum, a catcall in the corridor, even a proposition to pay me to sleep with them. This much testosterone on one campus is lethal.

So I keep my head down. I don't have the luxury of admiring Jude, their prodigy, or his eight-pack abs. Or the way his jet-black hair and clover-green eyes make him look like a panther stalking its prey ... both on and off the pitch. How his arms are so lean and muscled, they look like they can trap you in one place and venture to many unknown dirty areas ...

"You missed a stitch," Patricia points out as she walks past.

A breath escapes my lungs, and I mentally slap my brain to get it back into focus. And this is why I don't think about Jude Davies.

"I've just got to finish the Morley and Muncheiser lettering on the warm-up jerseys, and then I can call the distributor to talk about the fabric for the new rip away pants," I tell her since she is essentially my boss.

William rarely comes to the *sew house*, as everyone on campus refers to it. He stays in the main administrative building, where the admissions officers, headmaster, coaches, trainers, and other staff work during the day. The academy covers more than thirty acres, with ten buildings in total. There are the athletic facilities, consisting of weight, massage, spa, physical therapy, and film rooms that occupy two of the World War II era stone church-looking buildings. Three dorms, two buildings that house the academic classrooms the players learn in around four or five hours a day depending on their practice schedules, the main administrative building, a hall with stadium seating and a stage for presentations or social events, and the sew house.

Our building is the smallest and is set on the southernmost corner of the property. It's an old chapel that was expanded and outfitted as a tailor's shop. We sew, fit, clean, and repair every single article of match day clothing these players wear. While the big brands might produce the actual jerseys or gear, we customize it all. The player's names, their numbers, special occasion kits like those worn on Boxing Day ... every article goes by Patricia, Louisa, or me.

"He may really have cocked it up this time, though. Word is, Niles wants to trade him," Louisa muses.

"They can't trade him if he hasn't signed his official contract yet." The words fly out of my mouth before I can stop them.

Patricia raises an eyebrow. "Looks like someone knows more about Jude Davies than she lets on."

An annoyed huff blows past my lips. "Stop it. Everyone knows about that. People around here talk about Jude finally signing his pro contract as if it's the second writing of the Bible."

That much is true. There is always a buzz about when the owners and Harrington would offer Jude his real contract. Right now, he is on his academy contract ... which is still a cool three million pounds a year. But a player like Jude? His real contract is going to be epic. Like nothing British football has ever seen.

That is if he can keep it in his pants long enough to prove to the powers that be that he's worth all that money.

Not that I cared, or anything.

3

JUDE

"It's *mad* that you're back here, mate."

Kingston dribbles a ball idly from foot to foot, his skill so advanced that he doesn't even need eyesight to keep the thing in the air.

"A load of bloody bollocks," I agree, stretching my quads as the rest of the squad warms up.

After the cigarette scandal exploded all over the tabloids, Harrington chewed my arse out and sent me packing, all the way back to Clavering and the academy. It gutted me, although I would not show anyone that. I'll bide my time, wait a month or two until Niles realizes that the first team was losing too many matches without me, and he'll call me back up.

"At least you get to see us every day now," Vance says quietly, his pure mass making Kingston and I look like stick figures.

There is that. Kingston and Vance have been in the academy with me since almost day one. I was recruited first, Kingston, a left back, a year later, and Vance, our keeper, six months after him. Kingston comes from a line of footie players, his father is the great Edward Phillips of Italian soccer fame. The pressure to live up to his last name is even greater than the one sitting on my shoulders.

And Vance was pulled out a youngster league after a local coach noticed his intense ability. The chap is a brick wall of fierceness. There is a hardness about him ... something he doesn't talk about much but has also made him bloody brilliant on the field.

We've been inseparable since the time Kingston convinced us to toilet paper the headmaster's office when we were nine, and since then, we've been mucking up trouble everywhere we go. As we got older, pranks turned into nights out at the club, sneaking girls into our dorm rooms, street racing, and whatever other adult debauchery we can dip our hands into.

We are twenty-year-old phenoms with money to spare and talent in spades ... and the world is setting the stage to worship at our feet. Why wouldn't we take advantage?

"That's true, mate." I pat his arm, knowing he'd missed me.

Although cocky assholes in our own unique ways, we are brothers. These two are closer to me, even more so than my biological brothers, who I love very much. But Kingston and Vance understand what this life is like, which is a rare bond to come by.

"It's not fair, mate. You're the best player they've got, but Niles just gets pissy when you cock up. As if Luigi isn't out there screwing women outside his marriage, or Daton isn't sucking coke up his nose like a vacuum. And we all know Jasper is gambling away his entire contract at those underground poker tournaments." Kingston winds up and smacks the ball with his foot, sending it flying across the field.

Out of the three of us, his temper is the worst. Make him mad, and he's like a pit bull about to be put into a ring.

"Settle down, killer. If you fire balls at me like that today, I'll dye all your underwear pink. Again." Vance smirks a devilish smile.

A chuckle works its way up my throat. "That was brilliant, actually. Can you do it again?"

"Bugger off the both of you." Kingston flips us his middle finger as Coach Gerard trots out onto the field with his whistle.

Gerard runs most of the Top Squad practices here, which is the team the three of us are on. Top Squad is comprised of the players who are almost, if not already, ready to sign professional contracts and go play for Rogue FC in London. There are four or five more squads under ours, for those who will only ever play in second-tier leagues, or the kids who are recruited at a young age like I was.

Practice is grueling, especially on me. I'm never one to feel much pain when I play, and it is extremely difficult to get me winded. It's my biggest asset as a player to the trainers and squads I work with, I've even been called the Energizer Bunny. And no, I'm not going to make a dirty joke about how I could be called the same thing by the babes I shag ... that would be too easy.

But by the time Coach Gerard and the members of the best training squad are finished with us, it feels like I've been gut-punched repeatedly, that's how bad the running cramp is making the left side of my stomach seize up.

"Jude ... hang back," Gerard yells over the wind, the elements harsh on this blustery English landscape.

Kingston slices across his throat as if to say I'm dead meat, and Vance just gives me those pitiful puppy dog eyes he's famous for. I nod for them to go off without me, knowing they'll shower and then go back to our dorm suite to scream at each other over the latest edition of the FIFA video game.

My boots dig into the grass as I walk to my coach, head hung low, breath coming in spurts.

He puts a finger in my face, which is his first big mistake. "You're the reason every one of your teammates in there is going to be unable to walk for days. I am bloody sick of your shenanigans, Davies, as are a lot of other people within the RFC organization. If you don't get your act together, not only will we not be offering you your contract, but you will no longer be allowed to stay at the academy. Do you understand what I'm saying?"

Everything I do is under a bloody microscope. From the time I was seven, I was in the academy. When I turned ten, national papers and television stations started doing stories on me. They called me the next Killian Ramsey, said that I would bring honor and victory back to English football. Me ... a ten-year-old. Imagine having that kind of pressure on your shoulders?

And then, at age fourteen, my two baby brothers and I were left orphaned. Talk about pressure ... it was as if the whole of Mount Everest had been hoisted and placed down on my shoulders.

The media, my trainers, the lifestyle ... it molded me into the cocky, egotistical, prick I am today. It's how I survive. Drama, selfishness, havoc ... I thrive in it. Fuck it, if life was going to throw me shite, I was going to kick it and score goals.

I was going to be the fastest and most daring player, playboy, and man this country, or the world of international sports, had ever seen.

So, of course, I understand what Coach Gerard is saying. My career, my future, is on the line. And while the devil inside me is warring with the angel who barely got a word in, my brain, the logical part of me, wins over both of them. I know I have to straighten up.

"Yes, sir," I bite out but keep eye contact and my chin held high to let him know I am serious.

"Good. Dismissed."

4

ARIA

After finishing all the tailoring and stitching I needed to in the sew house, I set to work on my groundskeeping tasks.

Well, that's not exactly true. First, after my six-hour shift that finished at three p.m., I went home to cook, clean up, and administer medication. This is my normal routine, work the first leg of my day, go home and ensure that every single thing is in order and then go back for my second six-hour shift. Then I head home, clean up, and play nurse some more, fall into bed, and get up the next day only to do it all again.

Most would say it is no life to live ... but as I said, life or death here.

I plug my earbuds in my ears as I enter the athletic facilities building, armed with a rolling laundry cart and cleaning supplies. Every Friday night, I'm responsible for scrubbing down all three locker rooms that the numerous age groups rifle through each week. While my old mates from school are taking the train into London to dance their arses off at the hottest new nightclub, I am sponging dirty tile and plugging my nose as I throw the odd jockstrap into my laundry basket.

But it pays twenty pounds an hour, and at that price, I couldn't afford to say no.

Adele's "Hometown Glory" blasts through my ears, and I sing along, knowing that no one will hear me.

I only sing when no one can hear me because the last person to tell me my voice was worth something abandoned me at age ten.

But down here, in the empty locker rooms, as I go about my maid duties, no one is present to listen. I almost cherish this alone time, even if I am putting elbow grease into every motion. I've never minded cleaning and chores, and this is the only time in my life when I can let my hair down, sing, and let thoughts wander without worry or someone else chirping in my ear.

Lyrics are tumbling out of my mouth as I wipe each locker down with a disinfecting wipe, and then straighten and hang all the kits, clothing, and team merchandise within each. Then I move on to mopping the floor in this area, working my way toward the hallway, and into the shower area. The crescendo of the song has me raising my voice, testing out the falsetto that I only practice down here.

I let the beat take me, swaying my hips and getting lost in the emotion of it for a moment, dropping the mop in the bucket.

Someone clearing their throat, loud enough for me to hear over the music in my ears and my singing, has me jumping out of my skin. My body does a full one-eighty, freezing when my eyes fall upon the only other person occupying this space.

Jude Davies. Fully naked. Standing under the spray of shower water. His infamous blazing green eyes fixated on me.

My eyes eat him up, starting from the shock of black hair on his head, neatly trimmed but longer at the top. He usually swoops it back with gel to give his already intimidating persona just that much more swagger. Arms braced against the wall, long and lean with biceps that seem to flex as I flick my eyes over them. All of that caramel skin on display, from the way it stretches across his carved-in-stone abs, to the tapered set of his waist, to the bulging thigh and calf muscles, honed over years of running up and down the pitch.

I'm stuck to the spot, my mouth hanging open, no noise in the room besides the spray of his shower and the next Adele track humming in my earbuds. I rip them out, mortified and … if I had to admit it with a gun to my head, completely turned on. How could I not be? Here is the man who stars in probably ninety percent of adult British women's fantasies, standing in front of me with his long, perfect …

It's impossible not to stare at his penis. Because as far as penises go, and I have only ever seen one other this up close and personal, it's pretty spectacular.

I dated my secondary school boyfriend from the time I was fifteen, up until the day my life changed forever two weeks after my seventeenth birthday. My virginity was mine to give, and I'd gifted it to him as I thought I'd been in love. Turns out, cowards don't stick by you when your world goes to shit. Plus, he wasn't working with anything near what Jude Davies is.

The skin there is darker than the milky-coffee hue of the rest of his flesh, the veins thick and roping around the long member. A husky chuckle leaves his lips as he catches me staring, and I realize I've probably been looking at this man for a solid two minutes without saying a word.

"No one is supposed to be in here," I squeak, unable to pull my eyes from his nether regions.

Jude shrugs, a devilish smile gracing those full lips. "My roommate is shagging someone in our shower, and I wanted some peace and quiet."

"You can't have girls in your rooms." Random ideas are just tumbling out of my mouth at this point, apparently.

This makes him chuckle. "Would you like me to show you exactly how we sneak them in?"

Now he's sauntering toward me, completely comfortable with the fact that he's naked and dripping wet in front of a virtual stranger. What kind of superhuman specimen is this? He's perfect in every single way, from the small cleft in his chin to the golden shade of his skin, to the thick member hanging between his legs.

And now I do something really childish.

Slapping my hand over my eyes, I throw my other arm out, palm open and splayed, as if to say "STOP!"

Only, Jude doesn't. No, two seconds go by before I feel the smooth warmth of his chest, the muscles of his pecs pulsing under my fingertips. And when I peak through the hand shielding my vision, he's right in front of me, a wicked grin dancing in those surreal emerald eyes.

"I won't bite, love. Unless that's your sort of thing, of course."

"Oh my God." I swear, at this moment, my entire body flushes the deepest shade of pink imaginable.

Jude is still standing in front of me, knob blowing in the wind. Unless it's hard ... which I most definitely *will not* peer down to sneak a peek at.

"Your voice is brilliant. Do you sing?" Now he's in my face, trying to make me look into his eyes.

And I blush even harder. He heard me singing ... bloody hell. There I was, belting it in the men's locker room in the middle of the night, and arguably the most famous football player in all of England was standing there, naked, watching me.

The realization has me faltering, not that I wasn't before, but I'd been like a deer caught in headlights because *I'd* seen *him*. But Jude Davies hearing me sing? That is the utmost violation of my privacy ... it was the flicker of a dream I kept most secret.

That intrusion is the thing that snaps me out of my spell.

Backing away, I gather my supplies. "I'll come back when you're ... done."

"Hey—"

I turn on my heel and vanish before Jude can say whatever it is he was about to.

In all the time I've spent at Rogue Academy, I've always been able to keep my head down. To be invisible.

Except Jude Davies laid his eyes on me, and his skin under my fingertips. And now, I've never felt more exposed.

5

JUDE

My cock has never been harder.

Certainly, I've seen the intriguing blonde on the academy grounds a time or two. She's got a gorgeous, if not innocent, face. It's not one any red-blooded male would forget. She wears baggy clothing, to try to conceal those perfect tits I've gotten an almost-glimpse at a time or two when she bent down. Average height, desperately attempts to be invisible, all the while never realizing she's as forgettable as a bullet to the chest.

Every player here over the age of thirteen has been trying to subtly, and sometimes not so subtly, hit on her since she got hired about six months ago. In my time at the academy, I've seen a handful of attractive female employees come and go. The blonde is the hottest of them all.

So, it's no wonder that when she walked into the locker room, headphones in, belting at the top of her lungs and not noticing me ... it's no wonder my cock instantly perked up. It has been a whole week since I've had a proper shag, and my knob has been well-trained to stand at attention anytime a fit bird comes within twenty feet of it.

Too bad said bird didn't want to play. A shame really, because I could have shown her a *very* good time, alone in that locker room. It's a prime hookup spot of mine, as it is always deserted after seven p.m., and the room full of showers adds a bit of fun.

Whoever she is, she fled so fast that I hadn't even been able to get her name, much less convince her to take another long gaze at my proud cock.

Not that it mattered much ... I found out where she primarily worked in three seconds flat. Rogue Academy is my puppet, and I am its master; if I want something, it is given to me in less time than it takes to ask.

Which is how I end up outside the sew house at seven a.m. the next morning. I haven't seen this campus before dawn in a very long time, nor have I seen this building probably in that span either. The sew house is the one building I've spent the least amount of time in during my thirteen years at the academy. Once for a torn kit, and again to pick up my first team warm-ups that were made on a rush order before my debut game in London. Those were the only times I've been here.

Until today, that is. When someone filled me in that the blond girl who'd crashed my naked thinking session last night is one of Patricia's girls, I set my plan in motion.

Because I go after a conquest like a dog with a bone ... until I got my bone, that is.

As I walk in, the scent of coffee, metal, and something I can't place all hit my nose. And then, it's the explosion of color. I've forgotten what this building contains, as I haven't been here in so long. Rolls and rolls of material line the walls, with sewing stations dotting the open-concept floor plan. The hum of machines vibrate in the air, and Rogue FC gear hangs from every available surface. It's actually quite an enterprise ... and one the owners are smart to keep on premises.

"Blimey! Good morning, Mr. Davies." Patricia, the old woman who has run the sew shop since before I arrived at the academy, is visibly shocked as I walk into the room.

"Good day, ladies." I wink at the three women who occupy the room.

There is Patricia, who I recognize because she's basically as permanent as the tall oak trees that dot the campus quad. Another woman, mid-thirties maybe if I had to guess? But she looks older, and I've seen her try to cozy up to a number of my teammates.

And then, there is the blonde. The one with the husky, silky voice that seemed to stroke right down my cock as she belted at the top of her lungs in the locker room last night. Right now, she's staring at me with those big hazel eyes, the ones I haven't been able to get the long, thorough look I want at.

Without further ado, I walk lazily over to her station, and I don't miss how her tongue darts out to wet her bottom lip.

"Long time, no see, love." I sit down across from her on a rickety stool.

She has a pile of fabric in front of her, but I can see the way her hands nervously flick over the button she is sewing on a trainer's polo shirt. Her hands may be dodgy, but when my eyes scan her face, it's scolding.

"Do you need something?" The tone in her voice, like that of an annoyed mum, has me smiling.

"I'm Jude, by the way." I stick my hand out cheekily for her to shake.

She just eyes it, as if my fingers hold some wonky disease. "I have work to do."

The older girl, the one who is boring holes into my jaw like she wants to take a bite, answers the silent question I posed at the blonde. "Her name is Aria. And I'm Louisa, nice to meet you."

Yeah, I can tell she thinks it's nice to meet me. She'd probably let me bang her on top of her sewing station while these two watched if I asked her to. But I'm not interested. First off, she's too old for my taste ... eight years my senior? Nah, mate. Plus, her makeup is caked across her skin and she's wearing clothes made for a girl fifteen years younger than her.

I might not care *much* about who occupies my bed, but I don't shag desperate, tasteless women ... which Louisa over there clearly is. Might be harsh, but at least I have some kind of standard.

Also, since our shower encounter yesterday, Aria, whose name I've finally learned, is the only target I'm homed in on at this moment. Once she relents and falls into my bed—because let's face it, that's how this is going to end—I'll be instantly bored and abandon ever seeking her out again. But until that moment, I will pursue her with the strength of a Spartan warrior.

Turning my body away from Louisa, even though I can feel her and Patricia's eyes on my back, I lower my voice so they can't hear our conversation over the whir of the sewing needles.

"So, Aria, are you in the men's locker room every night?" The whisper accompanies my raised brow.

She sucks in a sharp breath, and I notice the small gap between her front teeth ... the flaw makes her more attractive. They're pearly white, as is her milky skin. But her cheeks, just round enough to make her look innocent while the rest of her body is sinful, are a subtle shade of pink. Her eyes aren't just hazel, either. They're flecked with olive and gold, a kaleidoscope of colors that have me staring deeper into their hypnotizing allure.

"Only on Fridays, when it's my shift to clean them," Aria answers, the air between us crackling.

Something about her answer, truthful and to the point, has

me wanting to dig deeper. While she may be stunned, she's not stuttering. Or flattering me. Those are typically the two responses I'm most rewarded with.

"And do you usually serenade the laundry and the toilets?" Because I'm genuinely curious.

Her voice is good. No, not good. Its professional-singer level great. She could be doing something with it … I've been around enough aspiring models, singers, and actresses to know that she possesses a voice better than any of those amateurs peddling their audition tapes around. Why is she here, slaving away at Rogue day after day?

"Keep your voice down," she hisses, and I lean back on the stool, impressed she has the bollocks to tell me off.

"Hiding something, Aria? I like a girl with a secret." She just made things way more interesting.

Seeming to remember herself, and our rank in this setting, Aria straightens. My eyes flick to her chest, the one she's trying to hide under a baggy grey sweater. But the article of clothing doesn't fool me. I can make out the swell of her tits, can practically feel how round and firm they'd be in my palm. Are her nipples pert and pink, like the shade of her cheeks? Are they full and a deep rose color, ready to be sucked?

Blimey, wouldn't *I* like to know.

"Unless there is something you are in dire need of, I really do need to get back to work."

Okay, I get the message. I'll let her get back to it. *For now.*

Standing, I slap the tabletop of her station lightly with my open hand. "It was good to learn your name, *Aria*. You know where to find me if you want to learn more. Or … I guess I should say, I know where to find you."

Her eyes go as wide as the saucer under a teacup, and I leave her sitting there boring holes into my back as I walk away. Just like she did to me last night.

6

JUDE

Being the three best prospects at Rogue Academy comes with advantages.

For starters, we are always served first in the cafeteria. I always get the best pick of the day's courses, and Kingston, Vance, and I are always reserved the best table. Being the best also means passing grades from teachers, preferential practice, and weight room times, extra massages from the physical therapist, and first dibs at new gear.

But the most rewarding perk we receive? The best dorm room.

Vance, Kingston, and I split a three-room suite on the top floor of the most central building on campus. That means our own spaces, even if we do have to share a bathroom. It has roof access, an entry point which is banned to students but we abuse anyway, and a service staircase that is essential to sneaking girls in. Our suite is also the only one with a big enough common room to fit a sofa in, and we've hosted many late-night drinking sessions that Coach Gerard would not be pleased about if he were to find out.

Kingston is lying on said sofa, a blue velvet sectional picked out by his interior designer mother, when he begins to whine.

"Let's go do something fun. Come on, it's Friday night. We should be out in London or something."

"Or at least down at the local pub." I nod in agreement, bored myself as I swipe through a dating app.

My body is draped over one of the puffy leather armchairs his parents sent, and Vance is making an imprint in the beanbag chair he brought back from home last Christmas. Our suite is a mish-mosh of upscale designer furniture from the Phillips residence, and mine and Vance's piss-poor homes.

Most of the girls on here have either been rejected on sight by me and the guys or passed through our suite at some point. Clavering isn't a big town, nor are the others surrounding it. The girls out here are slim pickings, and with London an hour and change away, the chances of some good female company tonight isn't looking promising.

I begin to wonder if Aria is on any of these apps. Or if I could find her on Facebook or Instagram. Without knowing the girl from a hole in the wall, something makes me think she probably isn't easy to seek out on the Internet.

"Clive would tell Coach Gerard, and then we'd be sat from tomorrow's friendly," Vance reminds us.

He's right. Clive, the owner of the Clavering Ale House, might like us enough. We've frequented his bar since we turned the legal drinking age of eighteen since it is the only establishment in twenty miles that served a pint. But he likes Gerard better and would tattle that we'd been out the night before a game.

"It's a bloody friendly, who cares?" Kingston whines.

Vance shoots him a death glare. "I care. I haven't been in goal for five weeks. I want at least some sort of competition, even if it's only against Haverforth."

Our mate has it tough. He's usually never called up, what with Remus Bayern being the goalie of RFC. Remus is an impenetrable force, he has five clean sheets this year already. While Vance is an excellent goalie, too, Remus is only twenty-five. He won't be leaving the net anytime soon ... which means Vance won't be called up. More likely, he'll be sold before he sees any playing time. It's just fate's nasty luck of the draw.

"Haverforth's academy is rubbish. A bunch of gits who can barely tie their boots. We could outscore them by five goals with three pints in us each." Kingston rolls his eyes.

He isn't wrong, Haverforth is a second-rate academy. The annual friendly between the schools is a tradition, if not a mean one. We gutted them year after year.

"So, like I was saying, let's cause some madness." That evil glint he got takes up residence in his eyes.

"Like what?" Vance asks, and I can see him start to relent.

Pranks and high jinks are our favorite pastime. Hanging the headmaster's extra suit from the flagpole? That had been us as thirteen-year-olds. Stealing Coach Gerard's nineteen forty-two bottle of rare batch scotch out of his desk drawer? We'd all had our first tumbler at fifteen and proceeded to wretch for hours afterward. Once we'd all lost our virginities, the prank always consisted of sneaking girls in.

"I downloaded some new porn. We could break into the main server room and stick a flash drive into the cable router? BAM! Bird-on-bird action for every lonely bloke tonight." Kingston grins.

For being a plonker when it came to basic math, our friend is surprisingly useful with technology.

And while it sounds like a hilarious plot, the threats stacking up against my future give me pause.

"I don't know ..."

My best friends went silent and turn to stare at me.

"This is worse than last summer, isn't it?" Vance asks, his eyes studying me.

No one in the room says what we're all thinking about. My DUI, the one I got last summer after a crazy night after leaving a club in London. It was my rock bottom, a stunt pulled on the anniversary of my parent's death that resulted in my face being splashed across the media for months. I had to go to court, where the worst that the judge had doled out was a bollocks ton of community service hours.

The public had vilified me for weeks, tweeting and commenting on every part of my life. Saying that I should go to jail, that I'd only gotten a slap on the wrist because I was a celebrity. Having to tell Niles Harrington had been akin to castrating myself. Having to tell my little brothers? That was a thousand times worse.

When I'd gotten into that car, I'd barely known my own surname. Thinking back, it was the worst decision I'd ever made ... but I was too much of a wanker to admit that to the public. So instead, I've been running amuck ever since. This was the time to be a plonker, wasn't it?

Apparently not. The conversation with Coach Gerard warred with the mischievous devil who'd always resided in my gut.

"I'm afraid so, mate."

Kingston shakes his head, throwing his hands up. "This is crap! You're the best player this country has ever seen. The second coming of Killian Ramsey! Shite, you're better than Killian. No offense to the god on earth who won us a World Cup. But come on, they can't do this to you!"

Rearranging, I swing around to sit with my elbows on my knees, facing them. "Thanks for your passionate support, brother. You're right, of course, but nothing I can do. You know the sacrifice, playing for my country, and we all know none of us would make it."

"So you're sidelined, essentially," Vance says carefully.

"When it comes to debauchery, yes." I hang my head.

Although, just as the words leave my lips, an idea sparks. I may not be able to get into my usual brand of trouble.

But there is another flavor of tumult I could dip my wick into.

7

ARIA

"Dad? I have your dinner out here, please come eat."

My voice hollers up the narrow staircase of our row home, the walls practically vibrating with my words. They're so threadbare, I can hardly believe they still stand day after day.

As I wait for him to slowly make his way down, I survey my work. His plate, set out on the table next to his armchair, in front of the TV. Healthy, yet tolerable food that hopefully he'll choke down and keep down ... at least until I'm home and can clean up any sickness that might occur. The remote, a glass of water, his crossword book, and cell phone sit beside the plate, all within his reach. The heat is turned on as high as I'm allowed to crank it without going over this month's allowance for our utility bill. The washing machine is whirring in the background, counters have been wiped down, the porch light is on so that I'm not spooked when I have to fish my keys out at midnight.

All in all, it took me less time today to set up for the next day than it did yesterday. That's something, right? All of this work means I'll have half an hour to relax in bed with my headphones in, listening to the newest Khalid album, before I pass out and start it all over again tomorrow.

"I could have popped a microwave meal in, you know." Dad's gruff but weak tone has me turning as he walks into our tiny living room.

"And I tell you every day, those contain way too much sodium. The doctor said lean proteins, vegetables, and healthy carbs. The best way to get you through this round of chemo is to give your body the best kind of fuel."

I may be speaking to him like a frustrated teacher, but it's only because I've told him this at least twenty times in the last month. He's on his fourth week of an eight-week chemo round, and it's been brutal.

Actually, the last two years have been a cruel kind of torture. When my dad got sick halfway through my third year of secondary school, it was as if my world stopped. The man who has sacrificed so much for me, who worked sixty-hour weeks in the steel factory near our house, who raised me single-handedly after my mother ran out on us, was diagnosed with lung cancer. I dropped everything; all of my activities, my friends, my boyfriend, none of it mattered anymore. The only thing in my line of vision was getting him healthy again.

Dad has been through a period of treating the cancer with medication, false remission news by a hack doctor we dumped days later, three rounds of chemo, more radiation than one body can handle, and a bunch of other procedures my brain wishes to forget. We've been in and out of hospitals, sat in more doctors' offices than one person should in a lifetime. While the medical bills might be covered, the rest of the expenses of life are not. And trying to keep up with them as a teenager, it was outrageous.

Is it any wonder I work myself into the ground? I'm trying to save my father's life. I'm trying to keep us afloat and pay the mortgage on this dingy, minuscule row home because he's been without work since he got sick. He took care of me by himself for years, busting his arse. It's only fair that I return the favor, now that he's the one with his back against the proverbial ropes.

"Rubbish ... can't a dying man get a steak? Or a Cadbury bar?" His thin, greying eyebrows raise in humor.

I point a finger in his face. "Don't you even joke about that."

"Come on, Ari dear, if you can't laugh at cancer, what can you laugh at?" He smirks, sitting down with a grimace in his old, plaid armchair.

My gut twists, because I know he's in so much pain. He went in for a dose today, and he hasn't puked yet, but we both know it's coming.

Choosing to ignore his dark humor, I sling my purse over my shoulder and slide my feet into the comfortable cleaning shoes I wear for my night shift. "All right, I have to go to work. You're going to be okay? Anything else you need?"

He crooks his finger at me, and I know he wants me to bend to him. My heart melts as I do because he places a chaste kiss on my cheek.

"You're an angel, my love. I'm going to be just fine. Now go, I don't want you to be late."

And I don't want to leave him, period. It has been far too long since I've been able to just sit and watch the telly with my father, to just enjoy his company without worry. How much longer can it go on like this? Are his treatments working? Is working myself to the bone eventually going to pay off? Will this be my life for the foreseeable future?

All the questions swim around in my head as they usually do, and it takes a look at the clock to shut them down. I'll have to sprint to the Rogue Academy if I am going to finish my tidying work at a decent hour.

I arrive at the athletic facilities winded and a little disoriented. With no money for a car, the insurance on it, or gas, I'm at least lucky that my workplace is only fifteen minutes up the road. But to get all of my duties done, I'm going to have to rush tonight.

So it's with a horrified shriek that I encounter Jude Davies, standing just inside the doors to the first of the football buildings I need to clean up.

"What in the bloody hell!" My hand flies to my chest, my heart beating double time. I'm almost an hour late, making it just about eight forty-five p.m., and the sun set over campus two hours ago. It's pitch-black outside, and in here, save for the odd corridor light that's been left on for my arrival.

"Did I scare you?" His smile is too smug and rehearsed for this to be a chance meeting.

"What are you doing here?" I demand, more than wound up about his surprise appearance.

It was bad enough he'd shown up in the sew house last week, a fact that neither Louisa nor Patricia had let go over the weekend. They practically jumped on me this morning again to ask about why he sought me out. I feigned ignorance and lied, said that Jude Davies had wanted nothing more than different stitching on his home kit.

I doubt they bought it, but I'd slipped my headphones in and gone to work, cutting the conversation short.

"Need to ask a favor, love." His lean, muscular form pushes off the wall where he'd been holding it up.

Bugger, he looks sexy. How was a guy allowed to look this dishy? Golden skin, biceps, and calves that could hold up a crumbling building ... he looks like some real-life version of the Hercules character in that Disney movie.

"Don't you pay people to do those?" I furrow my brow, annoyed that he's making me even later.

I don't care, *much*, that he's an international football star; he's making me miss my shift.

"Aw, love, don't I basically pay you?" Jude tilts that perfectly symmetrical head, pouting lips that have probably crooked up at more women than I can count on all my fingers and toes.

Now he's making me feel like some impoverished servant. "Yeah, we're done here."

Starting past him, I physically jump when his fingers graze my elbow. "Wait, I'm sorry that was prattish. I don't pay you, the owners do."

"You're about two seconds from me kicking you in the goolies," I warn him.

My day has been trying, and regardless of what pull he has at my place of work, I'm too exhausted to care.

"Do you want to go to London with me?" He smiles.

"You want me to ... what? I'm sorry, I must have misunderstood." *Blimey*, had he just asked me to go to London with him?

Was this reality?

"I need a ... handler of sorts."

Alarm bells start screeching in my brain, and I back away, holding my hands up. "Um, no ... I'm not that kind of woman."

Jude tilts his gorgeous head to the side, confusion marring those green pools, and assesses me. A second later, it's as if a light bulb goes off in his brain.

"You think I'm asking to hire you as a prostitute?" He delivers this sentence deadpan.

I shift uncomfortably, because yes, that is what I think. In fact, I think this superstar athlete has seen more than his fair share of prostitutes, and he's only twenty. The amount of indulgence he's accustomed to is probably more vast than I can even imagine.

When I don't answer, Jude holds his hands up, too. "I'm not ... Aria, I'm not asking you to sleep with me for money. Or to handle anything below my waist ... as much as that sounds like a brilliant idea. No, I don't need to pay for sex, if you hadn't noticed. What I do need is someone who will keep me out of any wonky business. Someone who will see a possible threat to my image and remove me from it."

"And you think I would be able to do that? Why? We barely know each other."

He shrugs, the cleft in his chin wobbling. "You told me to get out of the sew house the other day. Aside from Coach Gerard and Niles Harrington, no one says boo to me these days. Most birds fall at my feet, or on their knees. Most men want my autograph or to buy me a pint. But no one looks at me like I'm a bothersome fly on their arm that they want to swat. Well, except for you."

It's then that I realize Jude Davies is more pompous of a prick than I thought he was. Imagine having everyone around you kiss your arse from the time you were a school child? It's like he grew up in Buckingham Palace and has no idea how to act civilly outside the confines of it.

"I ... can't leave Clavering. Some of us have a day job. And responsibilities. Of which, I need to get back to." Grabbing my trolley of supplies, I try to move past him.

"I'll pay you ten thousand pounds for the two days I'm there." Jude shrugs.

I freeze; my face inches from him.

As if this kind of money is something he wipes his arse with. Rather spectacular arse it is, from what I've studied on the odd daydreaming moment when I've watched him out the window of the sew house at practice. Two round globes, sculpted and muscled enough to be visible under the tight football shorts ...

Focus, Aria.

That kind of money, to me, to my family? It could change everything. Ten thousand pounds could cover another couple of months of bills ... it could give us peace of mind. It could take the monkey off of my back, help me to breathe for just a minute without the paralyzing sense of dread crushing down on my lungs.

"*Shite* ..." I whisper to myself.

Jude Davies has backed me into a corner. And he knows it. Just throw money at something he wants and it works itself out, that's probably how he solves everything.

It was too bad, for my sake, that unfortunately, it was true here. "You're a smarmy bugger, you know that?"

"See, this is why I want you to accompany me to London."

I'd have to set everything up for Dad for a few days, but ten thousand pounds is ten thousand pounds.

"All right. When do we leave?"

8

JUDE

When I got the call from Harrington's assistant that they needed me in London the week after next, I thought it was a joke.

That reaction quickly morphed into smug glee, because he must really need me to play if he was having his assistant call not three weeks after he sent me back to the academy. And that emotion transformed into suspicion, because this may most certainly be a test.

To see if I can behave myself. To see if they can catch me with something, splash it all over the tabloids, and have a reason to sell me to another team. I'm not paranoid, I've seen stuff like this happen before. Niles Harrington isn't a dirty coach, but he was a ruthless tyrant when it came to the pursuit of winning the league. If I was enough of a liability, he wanted me gone now.

Which is why I decide to improvise.

If I am busy playing a game of cat and mouse with this Aria, then I'll be more focused on that than cocking up my future. My pursuit to get her beneath me would outweigh any daft decisions I might make.

When she'd hit me with the backtalk in the athletics facility,

I knew I'd made the right decision. And am now lusting after her even more than I had been before. Bloody hell, she was gorgeous when she got feisty.

We left yesterday, four days after I confronted her, to spend Friday and Saturday in London. Turns out, Niles wanted me back in town to ride the bench on Saturday afternoon's match. It was either a test to keep my head about me when I wasn't allowed on the pitch, or he really wants to show me what I'll be missing if I don't wise up.

Either way, I don't care. I can be a good ole chap, supporting my squad. The whole time, I'll be watching the friends and family booth at the top, wondering what Aria thinks about the Rogue stadium, the place that will soon become my second home.

She plugged her earphones in nearly the second we'd gotten in the SUV that would be taking us into London. I sat in the second row of three, in a bucket seat next to Barry as he went on and on about some new marketing campaign a sportswear company wanted me to be a part of. This meant I couldn't study Aria the whole drive as I'd wished to, because it would be way too forward to turn my body and stare at her in the back seat the whole time.

While I was persistent and cheeky, I wasn't desperate.

And I may not have been able to look her over, but it didn't mean I couldn't hear her music. A mix of The Beatle's, Drake, Florence and the Machine, Coldplay, Adele, and Lauryn Hill filled the silence of the car. The spillover from her headphones was just loud enough for me to hear what song she was listening to, and her song selection only made me more intrigued where it comes to Aria Lloyd.

Yes, I finally pulled her last name out of her when I had to make out the check for ten thousand pounds. *Before* we even left the Rogue Academy parking lot.

At this moment, I was waiting for her in the living room of our hotel suite, in one of my favorite places to lodge in Earl's Court. The hotel is upscale, a five-minute drive from the stadium, and a stone's throw from some of my favorite pubs and nightclubs.

Aria had almost pitched a fit when I told her we'd be staying in the same hotel room. Only when we'd gotten to the penthouse and she'd seen that I'd been teasing—the suite had three bedrooms—had she visibly relaxed. It made me wonder if she ever let her hair down, and how I could make her do so.

On the drive up, I'd wondered a lot about Aria Lloyd. Who did she need to take care of in Clavering? Was it a boyfriend? Not that that would stop me. Why wasn't she at university? She was clearly bright. Why take two jobs at the academy? Had she ever thought about singing professionally?

It scared me a touch that I even wanted to know so many things about her, when all this had started as a fishing expedition to get in her knickers.

The door to her room opens, and out she walks in a simple grey coat and black jeans, tennis shoes laced onto her feet. Any other bird I might have brought along would be dressed to the nines in red-bottom heels, leather pants, and a cleavage-baring sweater. No mind the cold for today's game, they would have gone for straight sex appeal and I would have salivated over it.

But something deep within me stirs as I see this innocent, fresh-faced girl step into our shared space. She's practical, unassuming, and has no idea how beautiful she is. Aria is only here for the money I'm paying her, and not because she fancies me in any sense.

"Ready to go?" she asks. "By the way, what are my duties for today?"

I never really laid out what I needed her to do.

"Well, you'll be in the box and I'll be in the seats behind the

Rogue bench, so … not much during the game. If I look up at you, maybe give your ole chap a thumbs-up for good behavior."

Aria rolls those shimmering gold-green eyes. "You're paying me ten thousand pounds to give you a thumbs-up?"

I shrug. "I've spent money on more ridiculous things."

"It's sad that I actually believe you. Or maybe it's more maddening that you have that kind of money to throw away. Have you ever heard of donating it to charity?" She huffs, picking up an apple from the bowl on the counter in the small kitchen of the suite.

I feel it when my face gets stony. "I donate a good chunk of my salary to various charities I feel passionate about. I may look like a pompous wanker, and even act like it, but don't act like you know where my money goes."

She's visibly taken aback as if she's just seeing the core of my being for the first time. Her head dips a little, her eyes softening. "I apologize. You're right, I don't know much, if anything, about you, truly."

Rolling my shoulders back and slipping that nonchalant charm back into place, I throw her a wink. "No worries, doll. Let's go."

9

JUDE

"You look ... smart." Aria's hazel orbs betray her polite words. She can't tear her gaze off my suit and that was my plan.

I'd promised to stay out of trouble when it came to the media. I never promised not to *cause* trouble with her. And when I told her we were going out for some celebratory drinks, even if I hadn't played in today's victory, it wasn't as if she could say no. I'm paying her to be here, to do basically anything I ask. Besides sleep with me, of course, because she'd already drawn the line that she wasn't a slag for hire.

And the way she looks right now ... Aria has trouble written all over her.

A simple long sleeve black dress that falls to her mid-calf hugs her body like a glove. It's the first time I've seen her out of those baggy clothes she wears while working on campus, and bloody hell was it worth the wait. Aria has the classic figure of a Coca-Cola bottle; round, supple tits stacked on top of a tiny waist which curves out into bodacious hips and a perky arse. I could run my hands down the line of her body and ride my fingers along the peaks and valleys. The dress is one that could have been pulled off the rack at any of those discount stores for teenage girls' clothing, but on her it's sinful.

"Didn't realize you'd have anything like that in your closet." My eyes rake over that body, two hot coals in search of somewhere to singe her.

Aria's chin drops to her chest, her gaze fixated on the hotel room floor, and I can tell that I've embarrassed her. Only, I'm not sure why. She's a bombshell, and I'm sure the local boys in Clavering have been nipping at her heels for ages.

"It's very old. Had to be dusted off. It's not … designer or anything." She still won't look up, curtains of golden hair swinging in front of her face.

Walking to her, my black custom-leather shoes tapping on the shiny hardwood, I invade her space. Instantly, Aria's shoulder rise with tension and I can see the barriers flying up behind her eyes.

A gentleman would have backed off, but I think we all know I'm not one of those. Sticking two fingers under her chin and pulling up, I make her look me in the eyes.

"No one said it had to be. You're a knockout, Aria. Not that you want *me* telling you that, but you are. Just because you hide this body under clothing ten sizes too big doesn't mean I haven't noticed it."

Desire has her irises dilating, I can tell. I know when a woman wants me, even if she won't admit it to herself.

Aria straightens, backing away from me. "What is it that you need me to do tonight?"

The grin that stretches my lips is wicked. "Watch my drinking. Weed out any slags who seem like they might cause a disastrous outcome for me. Alert me if any tabloid shite points their camera my way. Basically, keep me from going off the rails, but let me have a little bit of *fun*."

She clearly thinks she knows what my meaning of fun is

because those hazel eyes roll to the ceiling. "Do we have a curfew?"

"Oh, love, you've never gone out in London before, have you?" I tease.

"Actually, no, I haven't." Her answer is straight-forward.

Meanwhile, I almost choke on my tongue. "What? Have you been living under a rock?"

Sadness flickers through her eyes. "Something like that."

My heart twinges at her answer, and I'm surprised to find the organ I'd assumed was rotting, possibly isn't. And because of that, I don't ask her to elaborate.

Instead, I make for the elevator down to the garage, Aria silently following my lead, where a car takes us to one of the hottest spots in London at the moment.

Jet Lounge is one of the sexiest, low-key bars or clubs around the city. It's low lighting, velvet settees, craft cocktails, and tight-lipped policy draws celebrities and famous athletes alike. Which is exactly why I frequent it whenever I'm in town.

Aria and I walk in, the bouncer giving us a nod as I walk past the incredibly long line snaking down the alleyway where the entrance to the lounge is located. I purposely don't look back, grab her hand or graze my fingers over the small of her back. A moment of insanity possessed me back in the hotel suite living room, one where I *cared* about how she saw herself in my eyes.

That's not what this was about. I'm not looking for a bird to keep me; I am after one thing. Sinking my hard cock deep within her. And being pretty good at scoring, I know that eventually, with a brilliant game plan, I will win this game.

A drink appears before me, on a tray held by a gorgeous brunette waitress. Licking my lips, I nod my thanks and take a sip of the gin and tonic she brought over especially for me. There is a spacious rounded settee awaiting my arrival, toward the back. Each time I come here, the owner is kind enough to reserve me the best booth. *Ah*, the advantages of having a golden boot.

"Have a drink." I wave my hand at Aria as I spread my long limbs out in the booth.

"I'm fine, thank you." Her eyes flick over everything.

What must my life look like to her? "Oh, come on, no one wants to get pissed by themselves."

"I thought I was here to make sure you *don't* get sloshed."

The raise of my eyebrow should give her all the answer she needs. "Sometimes I say things and want you to do the opposite."

Aria is seething, I can feel it, and she still won't join me on the deep purple-colored velvet sofa. Her eyes leave their mission of burning the word wanker onto my forehead when sparks fly across the room. Dead serious, literal sparks. Some showy bugger ordered a flaming bottle of Dom Perignon, and I snort because this is so not the place.

I'm halfway through my second drink five minutes later, and Aria is still pacing in the space in front of my booth.

"You've really never been to London? Are you originally from Clavering?"

"Lived there my whole life." She confirms with a nod.

"And how have you never made the hour trip to the city?"

"Some of us are just country bumpkins, Mr. Davies. Though hard as that may be to believe."

I don't buy her answer for one second, because there is no truth held in her dazzling eyes ... even in the low light, I can make that out.

"Mr. Davies, huh? I'm not an old man, Aria. Barely older than you, from what I read in your personnel file."

Her mouth falls open. "You read my employee file?"

"Of course, I did, I wanted to hire you for a job. Couldn't let any random nutter into my inner circle. Now I think you might be too strict of a handler. One who is so serious, she won't even have a glass of wine with her charge."

"I take my job seriously, even if you're just paying me out of some dodgy, misguided pipe dream to get in my knickers."

This makes me chuckle because the girl holds no punches.

"Jude Davies."

Locating the person who just spoke my name, my eyes land on a tall, slim woman with a face that has graced billboards in London and New York alike.

"Celine." A wolfish grin shot in her direction.

Without invitation, the modeling industries current darling sidles up next to me on the sofa, her small knockers practically visible through the sheer sheath dress covering the essentials on her body.

The brunette skims her hands over the crotch of my pants, and I thrust out of instinct.

"They should have let you on the pitch today. I love watching you work." There is so much innuendo laced through her words.

My fingers trace the line of her neck, and I feel Aria's eyes boring into my forehead. "Some would say my best work isn't done on the pitch ..."

It's a typical industry encounter, fast and loose as if we're well acquainted enough for her to toss me off under the table in this lounge. There are no feelings, not even a mutual appreciation ... just sex and the awareness that someone will see us at this party and tell a reporter. At least we're both cognizant of the fact that this attraction is false, that this entire sequence of events is false theater.

Except when I look up from the imaginary trance Celine has me in, I see Aria's form, retreating quickly from my booth in the back of the lounge.

What in the bloody hell?

Before I can talk myself out of looking like a schoolboy

running after his puppy, I'm up and chasing her across the place. It's not until the hallway leading to the bathroom that I catch her, spinning in circles because she has no idea the layout of the building.

"What are you doing?" I swarm her, giving her no space to run.

Why my body and mind are possessed right now, to get up in her face, I'm not even sure myself.

"I need air," Aria bites out, squaring her shoulders at me.

"No, you don't," I challenge, backing her down the hallway as she tries to step away.

She opens those peach, pouty lips to say something, and then closes them again.

"You didn't want to see another woman's hand on my cock?" The words are dirty, but we both know they're true.

"You're a bastard." Her voice might be quiet, but it's steady.

"And a dangerous one, at least to a pretty little thing like you."

I watch as Aria backs herself into a corner, my arms pressing against the wall to bracket her head. "Why even bring me here at all?"

Against all of my better judgment, the question worms itself between the bricks I've constructed around my heart.

"There is somewhere I want to take you."

Then I take her hand in mine, the first time I've really touched her, and pull her gently out of the club.

10

ARIA

The venue might be small, no bigger than a room, but the dozen or so people staring up at me might as well have been a hundred thousand.

That's how bloody nervous I am. My palms are so slick, I can barely grip the microphone.

When Jude pulled me out of that god-awful lounge, his fingers lacing through mine, I nearly fainted. That's not an exaggeration, I was simply stunned ... almost as if I had whiplash.

One second, he'd been pawing some model in front of me, forcing me to look on as he openly seduced her. And the next, as I was walking away to collect my unnecessarily envious heart, the prince of English football was backing me into a dark corner, apologizing, and telling me he wanted to take me somewhere.

My foolish, girly head had thought that meant back to our hotel room. And I let him lead me away. As if I had no brain at all, just a damsel in some romance movie who blindly followed the rascal hero who'd given her no reason to trust him.

But ... I would be lying if I said I wouldn't have gone along with it if he had kissed me as soon as we'd gotten into the car.

What in the bloody hell is wrong with me? Lack of sleep and a new environment ... let's blame it on that.

I never expected, in a million years, that Jude Davies was actually taking me to an open mic night. Being discovered in the locker room whilst singing at the top of my lungs was something I'd tried to scrub from my memory.

Apparently, the gorgeous devil bothering me these days had not.

After the ride into London last night, one I spent entrenched in my music and watching new scenery out the SUV window, and the game today ... it seemed I couldn't escape him. Staying in the same hotel room, not to mention being thrust into his world without a parachute ... it was all a head rush. As if I'd stood up too fast and found myself in an alternate reality. Penthouse suites and chocolates on my pillow, box seats at the most famous stadium in London, a full-throttle football match that was more exciting than anything I'd ever watched on the telly. Chauffeured cars and catered meals, VIP club access and designer clothes I could never afford.

Gosh, had I felt daft in my twenty-pound Primark dress. And when Celine, a model whose face has graced my copy of Cosmopolitan more than once, strode up to Jude and put her hands all over him? I'd needed to smack myself back into reality.

I need to remind myself what I am here for ... the money. And who it was for ... my father.

But then Jude had gone and sucked me back in, crooking me around that debauched finger. Now, here I stand, about to sing for a crowd of strangers.

There is *no way* I can do this.

And then I find his face in the crowd, watch his lips as they mouth, "*let go*."

It was the last thing Jude Davies had said to me before he

pushed me toward the mic, his tall, dark form barely visible from the side of the stage.

"No one here knows you. Take this one chance to let go."

How this bloke, one I'm realizing I can't stand, knew the exact words to say to help build enough confidence in me to follow through with this, I'll never know. How he found this place ...

As the guitarist and piano player, the only two musicians on stage at this small venue, play the opening chords of my song choice, the realization dawns on me.

Jude Davies planned this.

He heard me sing, remembered it, and ... what? Found me a place to perform when I accepted his offer to accompany him to London? The idea is just too farfetched, but my gut tells me this isn't just a spontaneous gig.

The tune for Etta James' "I'd Rather Go Blind" hits me square in the chest, and keeping my eyes on him, I open my mouth to begin.

My lips move, words fill the air, and my heart gives itself over to the music. For the life of me, though, I can't seem to focus on anything else but Jude Davies.

Staring at me from a table in the middle of the room, a small smile gracing his lips. His eyes hold nothing but me in them, and for a second, it all melts away. The nerves, the worry, everything I've given up and all the insecurities I feel. When he looks at me up on this stage, like I'm the only girl he's ever seen, I feel ... powerful.

Something in my stomach dips, something in my heart gives way, and not only do I feel powerful, but I feel desired. I tip my head back as a big note swamps my vocal cords, drowning my body in sorrowful emotion.

The tragic heartbreak of the lyrics, the difficulty of the notes, both high and low, that a master like James nailed in this song ...

I hone in on them rather than the dinosaur-sized butterflies fluttering in my belly.

I've never done drugs before, only gotten pissed a handful of times with the responsibilities I'd taken on at such a young age. But I imagine the feeling of invincibility is something quite like this; heart in throat, head in the clouds, tingling limbs.

The weightlessness is so freeing that I could weep.

11

JUDE

The heel of her hand rubs at the spot in her chest that I know must burn with adrenaline. "Blimey, is this what it feels like to be high?"

My eyes blaze down on hers. "When I'm out on the pitch, thousands of people watching as I perform ... yes, it's the best kind of high. I know a way to keep that going. Trust me?"

It's the moment of truth. We've spent two days together, and while that might not be a sufficient amount of time to know a person, there is ... something indescribable here. Aria can see through this egotistical, prattish facade I put up for everyone else. The way she hands my shite right back to me proves it. She shouldn't trust me, not for all the jewels in the tower of London.

But after I heard her sing? No, not sing, it's too small of a word for what Aria's voice did.

That ability ... I've never heard anyone sound like her. I wasn't even aware of what the song was, but by the time she finished, I was bloody sure it was my new favorite.

Her tone was raspy but clear, soulful but could hit a high note that shocked your heart like a defibrillator. The way she played coy, with both the audience and the world around her in general, and then packed a musical punch so hard it could knock your socks off … I was fascinated.

"I want to keep it going."

In a single sentence, she puts her fate in my hands.

I shouldn't do this. Bringing her with me to London was specifically designed to avoid chaos such as this. But … Aria had just let it slip that she's never felt a high like this before. And besides playing in front of a packed stadium of thousands, there were only two other ways I've learned to have an out-of-body experience.

Shagging is off the table, that much I know. Pinning her against a mattress or taking her from behind up against a wall … that was my first idea. But I'm not pushing my luck, not yet.

So I'm down to the only other method I know that works for me; driving as bloody fast as I can in a really posh car. One call to Leonel, the upscale car dealer I deal with in the city, and a brand new Porsche 911 is delivered within twenty minutes. This is one of the outrageous perks to being filthy rich; you could call someone up at ten minutes to midnight and they'd have to procure whatever you ask for.

"How much does this car cost? No, on second thought, don't tell me. It's probably more than our house and my life savings." Aria runs her hand over the leather of the passenger seat and then moves those delicate fingers to the wood paneling on the dash.

"Who cares how much it cost? The question you should be asking is, how fast does it go?" Pressing my foot down on the gas as we're still in park, the engine revs smoothly.

"Maybe we shouldn't do this …" Aria's beautiful features twist into an expression of cautious doubt.

My fingers dance over the material molded to her thigh, and

her breath hitches. I knew it would, just like I knew that if I touched her, she'd succumb to my idea.

"Don't you want to ride the high?"

"Isn't this exactly what I'm supposed to be talking you out of?"

"But isn't it so much more fun to do away with what's right and go with what feels *wrong*?" I flash her my most diabolical smirk.

We answer every question with a question, and before she can answer, I ram the stick shift into drive and take off.

Zero to eighty in ten seconds and Aria has the complete opposite reaction to what I thought she'd do.

Most girls I take for a life-threatening thrill ride in a sports car ... they shriek the entire time. Make the whole experience as annoying as a public roller coaster and do that damsel in distress thing where they pretend to chastise me after.

But Aria Lloyd? While I can see her white knuckles gripping the sides of her leather seat, she doesn't make a peep.

Just lets the speed weave through her cells as I throttle us down the motorway, the whole time with a fiendish grin lighting up her entire face.

We're rocketing toward something monumental, and the excitement in not knowing whether we'll crash and burn or fly is the best kind of high. It's what I live my life chasing; that eye of the storm where uncertainty and possibility live immortally.

It's at the very moment that the high peaks, that I hear the sirens.

"Bloody hell ..." I mutter, the dread extinguishing my fun with a cold bucket of water.

"What?" Aria turns, probably too wrapped up in the joy ride that she didn't hear the police. "Oh. My. God. The police? No, no, no ..."

I can see her start to panic as I pull over, and I snap in front of her face. "Aria, shut it. Let me do the talking and calm down."

She is stunned, probably from being pulled over, and also from me telling her to shut it. But she does stay quiet.

Pressing the button to roll down the window, I come face-to-face with a pudgy Bobbie. "Officer, is there a problem?"

The twit studies his notepad. "Sir, are you aware you were going fifty kilometers over the legal speed limit?"

He hasn't looked up at me yet, but his line of questioning will change when he does. "I'm not sure it registered with me, no."

What's life if you aren't living it cheekily?

"Sir—" The officer finally looks up, and his words dry in his throat. I watch it happen. "You're ... you're Jude Davies."

"The one and only." I grin.

His mouth opens like a fish. Open and close, open and close. "You, uh ... you were speeding."

"I apologize for my behavior if I was doing anything wrong. But I've had a stressful day and wanted to rejoice in the victory of today's match."

"Brilliant match, it was. Shame you didn't see any playing time." The officer nods his head vigorously.

"'Twas a shame." I nod in agreement.

The policeman looks around, assessing the motorway up and down, and then bends down to the window of my car.

"All right, Mr. Davies, have a good night. Be safe, yeah? No more speeding ... except for out on the pitch. I expect to see you in the next FA Cup match, okay?"

"Righto, officer." I salute him and flash my best innocent smile.

He walks back to his patrol car and zooms off into the night, and I stay parked on the shoulder.

"I didn't mean to yell at you," I start, feeling the fury roll off of Aria in waves.

"I don't know why you like to risk your life or get into a spot of trouble just to have a good time, but I don't do this. You could have gotten us both arrested, or worse, killed. Your utter lack of regard for your safety or future is a posh man's problem, and unfortunately, not a luxury I have. I have someone counting on me, and I have to be alive to make sure the bills are paid and that life goes on."

I've rarely been made to feel a thing in the last ten years, and especially not anything akin to guilt or empathy. But maybe that's because no one has actually appealed to those emotions in me. Everyone around me is just as much of a careless adrenaline junkie as I am ... or that's just who I've chosen to surround myself with.

But right now, I feel like a real wanker. And I'm not such a prick that I don't see how upset, or irate, she is

"Aria, I apologize—"

She cuts me off. "Save it, Jude. I just want to go home, back to Clavering. Can you make that happen?"

I nod, unlocking my cell and calling whoever handles that kind of thing to send a car straightaway. We sit in silence on the side of the road, the sports car's mighty engine of no fun to me now.

"Listen, this is not how I meant for this to go," I speak into the void.

Her cornsilk hair tumbles down her back, her face is turned away from me. It doesn't flutter over her shoulder, because she never faces me.

"We're just from two different sides of life. It was reckless for me to even accompany you as an assistant when I have duties to see to back home. Don't ask it of me again."

"Got it," I say, so that she knows I understand.

It takes another five minutes for the car to get to us. Five minutes I spend with a sinking feeling working its way through my heart and stomach. I may have proposed this trip as a way to get closer to Aria, to seduce her into sleeping with me.

But as it's ending in horrible fashion, I realize, she may have seduced parts of me I wasn't aware even existed anymore.

12

JUDE

"I don't understand why we still have to go to classes. We're twenty bloody years old ... and in another life, I'd never be caught dead at university," Kingston complains.

"Lord knows you aren't smart enough to even get into university," Vance quips, setting his books down on the desk.

Out of the three of us, Vance is clearly the least thick. And I say that because none of us is Oxford-level genius ... from the moment we were born, we were meant to play football. But our keeper can at least do simple math, understands the laws of physics, and schools us all on the required reading we're supposed to do. I say supposed to because I haven't cracked open a paperback or textbook in nearly two years.

"That's right, because I'm not *meant* for it. I'm *meant* to be out on the pitch or in the weight room ... this is mad." Kingston points to the front of the classroom where one of the professors sets up the presentation he'll drone on about for the next hour.

I won't be listening. My vote is on Kingston's side for this one; higher education classes are a waste of my time. I barely made passing grades when I was in the secondary school level at the academy, and those were required if I wanted to play. Most of my schooling time has been done in the academy since I arrived here so young. And while they claim, to outside parties and sources, that the education here is top-notch ... it is the worst-kept secret that football takes top priority. The classes are rudimentary, and professors slip passing grades into the pile so that the future players of England's National Team can bring the honor and victory they were bred to bestow upon the country.

So yes, it is rubbish that we have to continue with university courses while we are stuck in the academy.

But today, my mind is elsewhere anyway ... even from this conversation, the thousandth we've had on the subject of schooling after the age of eighteen.

No, my thoughts are occupied by a certain Clavering blonde who ghosted me a week ago. Ever since I almost got her involved in a traffic violation that, if it had been any other person in the driver's seat other than England's resident football bad boy would have landed her in custody.

"Hey, how was London, anyway?" Vance practically reads my mind.

"And how come you didn't tell us you were taking the sexy sew house girl? When did you finally land that hard-to-get bird? Lucky bastard, she's smoking." Kingston hits me in the arm.

I flip open a notebook and begin to write down the film I want to view in the athletic facility's small theater later today. The entire match from Saturday, that's for sure. I want to watch what the opposing team's forward did on a penalty kick that netted them a goal against us. The little flip of the ball with the toe of his boot was interesting—

"Earth to Jude? The sew house girl?" Kingston interrupts my thought.

"How did you wankers find out about that?" The idea flicks me in the temple like a sharp rock thrown at my head.

"Vance found some pictures of you and Celine on Twitter

from Saturday night. Sew house girl was in the corner of them. At first, I thought it was some photoshop joke, but then I thought, 'No one knows who that babe is so ….'" Kingston shrugs, looking for me to fill in the blank.

"*That babe's* name is Aria, and she was there as my … assistant." I shoot my best friends an annoyed look.

"You have an assistant now? For what? Schlepping your luggage whenever Niles sends you back down?" Vance snorts, looking down at his own notebook.

The middle finger on my right hand flips straight up toward him.

"Fuck off. She … she intrigues me. Only way she'd get near me was if I offered to hire her." I hold up a hand as soon as Kingston starts to speak. "Not like that, you twit. Aria is not like the girls we normally encounter, and she certainly wants nothing to do with me besides a professional relationship. To be honest, I only asked her because I wanted to shag her … but it's not going to happen."

"Damn, well, I guess you found us the answer we've been searching for the last six months." Kingston squeezes my shoulder in a conciliatory gesture.

There has been a running bet between some of the older academy players about who would get Aria between the sheets first. Needless to say, we are a bunch of randy young men who attended an all-male school and get off on speculating about such juvenile things.

Except now I know that no one will ever win it. Well … except maybe me. There was a moment there, in the dark corner of the back hallway in Jet Lounge, where I could have done anything to her. I could have bent down and tasted her lips, I could have suggested we go back to the hotel.

I'd felt it after her performance at the open mic night, too. The one that a low-level A&R man had been attending, seen me, and asked who Aria was. Not that I've been able to tell her this past week ... she has been avoiding me like the plague. I can easily get her phone number, it is in the employee file Barry secured for me when I decided to take her to London.

But, Aria needs time to cool off, that much I know. If I wait for the precise moment when she is weakest, I could exploit it to my advantage and cull out that wild streak I'd seen in her.

That is the girl I want to know more of. She is the one who would have let me fuck her next to the loo entrance in a VIP club.

There is more to it than that, even if my wicked heart keeps on denying it. I want to make her wild, yes. It's the unanswered questions that nag at me worse than the need to corrupt her, though.

Why do I get the feeling she's never been on a stage before?

Why has she never traveled to London before?

Who is in Clavering that she needed to get back to attend to?

Why was a pretty nineteen-year-old slaving away at Rogue Academy?

The mystery that is Aria Lloyd has me intrigued. For the first time ever, I want to know just as much about what is going on in a woman's head as what is going on beneath the zipper of her trousers.

13

ARIA

In the week since I came back from London in the middle of the night, life has returned to its normal, torturous monotony.

No exclusive clubs, celebrities, fast cars, or dangerously hot villainous men to be seen. Just my grueling hours of work, followed by grueling hours of home care and dad's treatment schedule.

The reason I never do anything for myself, like sing in front of crowds or allow a crush to sprout hope in my chest? Because when they're stolen back, taken by the cold, clutching fingers of fate, it's that much more disappointing. It causes that much more heartbreak.

I've been allowed to see how the other half lives. What it feels like to view money as no object, and how it is to live freely, wildly. Not even before my father's diagnosis was I allowed to gallivant throughout my days so carefree. I have a mother who left me; I have an invisible pain in every fiber of my being.

Maybe I knew once what it was like to have the possibility of a regular life, one with friends and school and a job you picked because you sort of fancied it ... but that option is gone.

It had only been foolish and masochistic of me to dip my toe in Jude Davies' pond.

Once again, I'm back in the men's locker room, scrubbing it down after an already long day. One made longer because of the routes I had to take all over campus to avoid seeing said villainous man.

The bloke is too good looking for his own good, or anyone else's. I have to stop thinking about him, and fast. Each time his face pops into my mind's eye, my heart skips a beat. Which is daft and girlish and makes me feel like a bloody idiot.

"Shite, I wanted to get here first!"

The deep voice makes me jump, even over the sound of Alicia Keys singing "Fallin'."

Standing in front of me is Jude, dressed in jeans and a plain white tee too scandalous for public wear, but only on him. How did he manage to make working man's clothes look like an ad for some sexy, sexed up, sex club?

"What are you doing here?" I click off my music, furiously pulling the earbud from my right ear.

"I'm here to apologize. See, I even kept my clothes on to make you feel more comfortable." He waves his hand down his body.

As if the clothing covering all of his beautiful bits makes me less immune to the godly body he possesses.

"Not bloody likely ..." I mutter to myself more than him.

Jude tilts his head. "You'd rather me disrobe? That would make you more comfortable? Okay ..."

He shrugs and lifts his T-shirt up a fraction, revealing olive-toned skin stretched over washboard abs.

"NO! No, please keep your clothes on, thank you!" My voice is squeaky and frantic.

All I wanted tonight was to be alone and get this done quickly. And now the one person I never wanted to see again is here. Realistically, I know working at Rogue Academy, I am bound see him. I'm not completely mental. But Jude will someday soon be gone to London for good, and I'll be here, in Clavering, surviving. It stands to reason nothing good can come from this flirtatious dance we are doing. Teasing your hand over the flame, nine times out of ten, will leave you burned.

"Okay, don't get your knickers in a twist. Or do." Jude winks those gorgeous green eyes and I frown. Even when he claims to be apologizing, he's a hornball. "I'm here to say sorry. And the best way I know how to do that is to help ... so let me help."

I stare at his open hand, wondering what he wants me to do. "You don't need to apologize. I'm a big girl and have work to do. So, could you leave me to it? Thanks."

"Aria, I'm going to help you. So that you can finish faster."

His words aren't an innuendo but with the way my core flushes, they might as well have been.

My brows raise. "Do you even know how to handle a mop? Or a broom? Or wipe down toilets?"

Jude scuffs one sneaker against the other. "Well ... not technically. But I'm an excellent student."

Again, why do I have the feeling we're not talking about cleaning a loo? Still, I can't deny that it would be nice if he cut even five minutes off my chores down here. Five more minutes I could spend sleeping or writing those new lyrics that have been floating around my head for three days.

"Fine. Take this mop and start over near the sinks." I relent, shoving it into his hands.

We work in silence for the next fifteen minutes; me working as efficiently as possible, and Jude trying to cover every minuscule centimeter of the floor with polish. No wonder the man is a football player, he probably wouldn't make it in the real world.

"I really am sorry, Aria. I never meant to get you into trouble or take risks with you as you called it. The only thing I was trying to show you was a good time. Which I think you were having before the Bobbies showed up?"

His question hangs in the air as I contemplate his apology. "It doesn't matter, anyhow. I told you, I don't really have time for all of that. There are more important things I need to tend to."

"Why did you even agree to accompany me to London? You knew I was only asking as a tease. You knew that I was trying to bed you, and yet, you still went."

And this is the vital difference between us. He's so wealthy, so revered and rewarded for athletic talents that were ingrained in him the minute he was born—say what you want about hard work, you can't teach the kind of talent Jude Davies has—that he doesn't even register how much ten thousand pounds means to someone like me. Where he doesn't even bat an eye, that kind of bankroll could help us eat and live for the next half a year.

"My father was diagnosed with lung cancer almost two years ago."

Speaking the words out loud feels like thousands of tiny glass shards working their way out of my throat.

Jude's hands stop maneuvering the mop, but he doesn't look at me. "And that's why you take on extra shifts?"

I nod, even if he can't see it. His back is still toward me. "We need the money. I'd work day and night if it meant I could keep him comfortable enough to fight admirably."

"Is he on government wages?"

"He wasn't working at the time of his diagnosis, so the government has been less than helpful." The steely tone to my voice is directed at the local officials and his former employer who've tried everything to screw an honest man out of financial help.

"And your mum? Does she work?"

When I stay quiet for too long, Jude finally turns to face me.

He looks ... angry. I'm not sure why, but the expression on his face could scare Godzilla.

"My mum left us when I was ten. Decided she'd had enough, walked out in the middle of the night, and we haven't heard from her since."

"*Bitch*," he mutters under his breath.

I shrug. "While that may be, dwelling on it isn't going to save my father's life. The only thing that will is chemotherapy, and me keeping our household afloat while my father isn't able to work. So, that's why I agreed to go to London. I needed those ten thousand pounds."

Jude is silent for a moment, and I see the shift in his eyes as it happens.

"I know what it feels like to be the sole earner in your family ... even as a teenager. When I was ten, I signed my first contract with the academy. It was amateur, and obviously nowhere near the amount of money I stand to make when I turn pro."

I don't interrupt to ask when he'll stop cocking up so that he *can* turn pro, but I think it. Someday, if I'm brave enough, I should confess how daft I think he is for spoiling so many chances to get out of Clavering and stepping onto the world stage.

"But the pounds laid out at the bottom of the sheet they had me sign? I remember my mum crying at the conference room table. It was more money than she and my dad made in a year, combined. And that was per quarter. At the time, I barely had an idea of what that meant. I didn't realize I was helping to clothe, feed, and shelter my family. It never dawned on me that because I was given a mythical right foot and a good work ethic, that my family could stop living paycheck to paycheck. At least, not until I began to age up. And then, after the accident ..."

This bold, cocky, *sensitive* man trails off, and I know he's thinking about his parents.

Then the walls come back up, he puts on the showman's facade and brushes it all away. "Anyway, I won't ask you to have fun again. You can count on that. I wanted to say sorry. I hope I've shaved some time off of your shift."

He hands me the mop and walks out of the locker room.

I'm left standing there, wondering how the roles have just been completely reversed. Because now, I'm thinking I should go track Jude down and comfort him.

14

JUDE

Two days later, the conversation I had with Aria in the locker room still haunts me.

I don't talk about my parents, not even to Kingston and Vance. Their deaths made me an adult in the way only the status of orphan being painted on you can. From the moment the passenger train they were on derailed, killing a dozen and wounding hundreds more, my life took a sharp left and veered down a track I'd never realized was there.

The academy had come calling when I was seven, and I'd lived there for seven years already when the headmaster and two of my coaches came to tell me that my mum and dad were dead. I remember thinking it was some kind of joke, that they were talking rubbish. I didn't break down until ten minutes later when one of them had to pull up the news story online to show me the photos of the crash. And my parents' photos beside pictures of the wreckage, listing them as two of the dead.

From that moment on, there was only life before their deaths and life after. We'd grown up middle class, and while I'd still lived at home, we'd never struggled too much. My brother Paul was born six years after I was, and Charles followed two years after him. Rowdy, incorrigible boys, our parents loved and scolded us equally. When Dad discovered I was more than decent with a football, he signed me up for lessons. I caught the eye of a scout not a month later.

School was paid for, as was a stipend the club sent to my parents in good faith of my future success. To an outsider, the whole process probably looks like some kind of child trafficking scheme, but this is how players are bred. My parents knew that, and I never complained about how hard I was pushed or how difficult being a young child in the academy was. I craved the life more than anyone ... I wanted to grow up and be the next international football legend.

But when my parents died, all of that changed. It wasn't exactly something I had to do for myself, but my career and path became about supporting my two younger brothers. Luckily, my mother's sister and her husband took Paul and Charlie in to care for them day-to-day. I, though, felt the need to provide financially. Half of every paycheck I received from the amateur contract I'd signed went to my brothers. When I eventually signed my multi-million-pound deal to go pro, I set up trusts in their names so that they'd be set for life.

Our parent's deaths may have hit me the hardest, as I'd spent the most time as their son, but my brothers had been with them every day. They were only babies when they died, had no experience out in the real world like I did.

So, it's no wonder that after talking to Aria about them, I am all cocked up in the head.

And drowning my sorrows in loads of alcohol.

"That wanker!" Kingston storms into our dorm and throws his knapsack across the room.

"Hello to you, too." I nod, lifting up my beer in welcome.

It might be a Tuesday night, but I am halfway through a six-pack and have some gin in the freezer that is calling my name.

Alcohol loves misery, after all.

"What are you yelling about?" Vance comes out of his room in nothing but boxers, rubbing his eyes.

"Were you asleep in there? I had no idea!" I chuckle, half-pissed already.

"Are you drunk?" His sleep haze has him looking confused.

"Headmaster Darnot is a complete and total wanker!" Kingston is still yelling, which apparently, my sloshed-self thinks is hilarious.

Vance crashes down on the sofa beside me. "Are you drunk?" Then to Kingston, "What did he do now?"

"The bastard gave my parents an 'update' on me." Kingston throws his tatted arms up, the exact reason his parents keep such a close eye on him literally painted on his skin.

Kingston is one of the football world's golden children. I literally mean precisely that, because he is the offspring of the former Italian keeper who won them a World Cup, and a Swedish woman footballer who brought back Olympic gold to her country. The Phillipses are a football dynasty, and their son had no other choice but to follow in their footsteps.

Anyone would feel sorry for me, what with two dead parents, but sometimes, I almost feel worse for Kingston. I play football because there is simply nothing else I want to do. It's in my blood, it feeds my soul. He is forced into it. Even if he loves the game, loves being out on that pitch, he was still pushed into the sport, gave no consent to having his future planned out for him.

I feel even worse, that because of who they are, his parents are granted special meetings with the headmaster to talk about Kingston's on the field and off the field success.

"Get pissed with me!" I hold up my empty beer and venture off into the kitchen to grab another.

"Nah, I'm too angry to drink. If I have alcohol now, you'll have a recreation of Boxing Day twenty fifteen."

Vance and I both shudder remembering the night. Kingston had just arrived back from holiday with his parents, frustrated and ready to lash out. Long story short, the night ended with our friend throwing the majority of our furniture out the dorm room windows, which he'd first smashed. Priceless antique glass windows, some of them stained from artists long dead, that his parents had ended up having to pay for.

"All right, what are we doing then?" Vance sighs, going back to his room to, I assume, put clothes on.

"Let's egg Darnot's office door."

Rolling my eyes, I take a long pull from my new ale bottle. "Come on, that's primary school tomfoolery."

"Well, maybe I'm feeling extra juvenile today, humor me." Kingston shoots me a death glare.

"Can we just get on with it? You're going to argue for fifteen minutes about what prank we should pull, and in the end, you'll both land on egging his door because we're old and lame and it's a Tuesday. So let's get a move on because I want to go back to bed."

Vance is standing in the doorway, our suite keys in his hands, ushering us out the door.

I shouldn't do this. I've been successfully avoiding trouble for months, or weeks, that my friends knew about. My future is on the line, all that I want to accomplish hangs in this moment. I shouldn't go along with them ... and yet ...

That creeping feeling of being rotten to the core, the one that fuels us to act on the tainted parts within us, put there by Adam and Eve, cheers me on. As I picture those eggs cracking against the dark wood door, a devilish glee fills me. Pair that with the too many drinks I've consumed and no part of my rational brain was ever going to win.

"Yeah, all right, fuck it." I toss back the rest of my bottle and slip trainers on my feet.

"The merry band of bad boys!" Kingston shouts as he follows us, rubbing his hands together like a villain.

15

ARIA

Working at Rogue Academy for over seven months now, I'm beginning to learn the secrets of the centuries-old campus.

First, there is the tunnel Louisa showed me in my first weeks, the one underneath the film room in the athletic center that travels all the way to the lobby of one of the younger boys' dorms. Then I found the tiny chapel built into the side of a hill on the north end of the academy's acreage. It is no bigger than an olden-day natural pantry but has an altar and two pews nailed to the earth.

The charm of the academy could be lost on those who didn't look for it, and most days, I didn't. But if you stop and stare for a moment, the history here can astound you.

That's why every lunch break that I decide to stay on campus, you'll find me in my favorite hidden spot.

When I do choose to take the rare hour for myself, to eat and listen to music, I tend to go to the bookcase in one of the back rooms of the administration building. Being the campus janitor gives me access to every room at the academy, and while I'm dusting or mopping, I often find a lot of the secret rooms or tunnels by pushing or pulling on random fixtures too hard.

I found this passageway two months ago when I was picking up the books and knickknacks cluttering the shelves. I tried to move a copy of a Dickens' novel, and suddenly the bookshelf creaked away from the wall. It had given me such a fright that I nearly fainted. Being the big fat chicken I am, there was no way in bloody hell I was going to go down there that night. Alone, in the dark … no chance!

However, I went back the next day on my lunch break and explored. Turns out, it is a tunnel that leads to the cafeteria building. However, along the way, there are little alcoves, carved out like big, circular, concrete daybeds that are perfect for relaxing in peace.

On rainy days, or any other day, this is my favorite spot. It's private, hidden, and quiet.

I've just taken a bite of my brought-from-home tuna sandwich when a sound coming my way spooks me so badly, I smack the back of my head on its concrete resting place.

"Ouch …" I rub the tender spot.

"Aw, *come on* …" Someone's voice trails through the tunnel, as they must hear my music and see the little light.

And who but Jude Davies appears just seconds later. "Aria? I thought you were going to be a primary schooler, in which case I would have told you to scram. This is my teatime spot."

"This is *my* lunch spot." I fold my arms, not standing up.

I'm not sure why I'm picking an argument when he ended our last encounter with an apology. If anything, I've been thinking about him for the last four days, and how I should show him some sign of kindness. It isn't often that Jude speaks about his parent's death … he barely addressed it in the media in all the years they've been gone. I get the feeling, from hearing him speak about it the other night, that it is extremely difficult.

Obviously, when would something like that not be awful to explain? My mum had merely abandoned us, not died, and I couldn't form words on the subject.

"Then how come I've never seen you here?" Jude leans against the wall, his form dwarfing my hidden spot.

I begin to pack my bag up. "It's ... not every day. But I get a lunch break at noon and if I don't want to waste half an hour of it running home and back, I eat here."

"I usually eat here around one, right after practice. I wondered who kept leaving crisp crumbs everywhere." He grins. "Stay, please. You looked relaxed."

Staying seated as he asked, I try to roll my shoulders to get the tension out of them. It doesn't quite work.

"Aria, I can go if you don't want me here." Jude's eyes pierce me.

"I don't not want you here. You just ... I didn't expect to see anyone down here, okay?"

He smirks. "You forget that I've been roaming these tunnels a lot longer than you have."

"Yes, we get it, you're Mr. RFC himself."

"Got that right, love." Jude grins as he moves toward my alcove, drops my bag to the ground, and sits right next to me.

I pick up my bag of crisps and pop one in my mouth, feeling awkward and not knowing what to do next.

"How is your day going?" Jude asks, eyeing my sandwich.

I roll my eyes, because *men and food*, picking up the uneaten half and handing it to him. He starts chomping away happily.

"It's okay. I'll go back to the sew house for a bit and then home, then come back to clean the facilities."

"You do this every day of the week?" he asks.

"Aside from Saturday and Sunday. Although, sometimes, I'll pick up a cleaning shift on those nights." The sew house is closed during the weekend.

"That has to be exhausting." He meets my eyes.

I shrug. "It is what it is."

The alcove we're sitting in is cramped, and when Jude polishes off the sandwich and rubs his stomach in a satisfied motion, his shoulder brushes mine. Instantly, tingles erupt all over my body. An ache begins between my legs, one I'd never known resided there. As I look up, my eyes catch Jude's, and I gasp to find that his are fixated on my mouth.

I know what it's like to kiss a boy. I even know what it's like to have sex with one. But my lord, I have never felt a pull or desire as strong as this.

Using every last ounce of effort I have in my body, I force words out to try to extinguish the burning.

"When I told you about my father, you didn't offer to help," I point out, still stuck on this thought from days ago.

"Because you wouldn't have taken the money, no matter how much I want to give it to you. You're too proud, a characteristic I find commendable. But I also know your plight too well. You are the one who holds up your household, it would be an insult to try to give you resources rather than just applaud your hard work. I didn't ask, because I knew it would make you feel like charity. And just so you know, I've never thought of you that way."

His answer fills me with the simplest, most powerful form of appreciation I've ever felt. Out of everyone in the world, the last person I would expect to get my mentality so thoroughly would be Jude Davies. And yet, here he sits, inches away from me, practically spelling out my thoughts.

We must move at the same time, if not me a split-second faster. Jude's lips meet mine in the middle, and the minute they collide, I swear, it's like fireworks detonate between us. His skilled mouth clamps down on my own, manipulating and working torturous circles around every single cell my lips are made of. The small tunnel's air temperature is too humid, the alcove about to explode with the heat our kiss is putting off.

Why did I try to trick my mind into thinking that this wouldn't be life changing? That kissing Jude would be mediocre, or okay at best?

It's as if my heart, my sex, every wanton need in me no longer resides in my body, but instead has meshed with his. The kiss is dirty, teeth and tongues everywhere, but sensual at the same time, with Jude laying small pecks on the corner of my mouth or cheeks at intervals. It seems to stretch on forever, and time warps or stops ... I'm not really sure.

I *am* sure that Jude begins to push my sweater from my shoulders, and I let him.

"I hate that you cover this body." He groans into my mouth as he cups my breasts through my shirt.

Sighing into his mouth, I push my shoulders together, thrusting my chest farther into his big palms.

And right when as he's about to pull his lips from mine, and I suspect plant them on the spot on my neck that is begging for him ... his phone starts to vibrate against my thigh.

And even though I'm silently screaming for him to ignore it ... he does the thing that self-assured twits do and goes to answer it.

"Bugger ..." Jude whispers, looking down at his cell phone. "I have to go. But ..."

But what? Is he going to ask to see me later? To talk about this? Coming from a guy like Jude, I'd never expect that.

"I'll find you later, okay?"

I don't believe him, not for a second, and I wouldn't put it past him to have faked that phone vibration as a way to escape answering questions.

All I do, however, is nod. Because he's rendered me speechless.

Because I finally know what it is to be put under Jude Davies' full spell.

Because I'm afraid that if I speak, I'll ask him to kiss me again.

And that's the kind of thing that leads to trouble.

16

JUDE

"You're aware the nature of the conversation you had with Coach Gerard a month ago?"

Headmaster Darnot sits perched in his leather high-back chair, a tiny man with a, probably, tiny willy trying to grasp at power.

"Yes." My voice is clipped.

"So you know that throwing eggs at my door is an offense punishable by kicking you out of the academy?"

I stay silent, not about to incriminate myself.

"I know that it was you, Mr. Phillips, and Mr. Morley. We installed security cameras above the entrance to my office the third time you boys did this. We're not that daft, as much as you might assume we are."

Well, it took them three rounds of us egging the headmaster's door to finally install a cheap surveillance cam, so yes, I did think they were rather daft. But I wasn't about to say so.

Darnot stands, pacing in front of his chair like some evil dictator about to give a monologue of his devious plan. This is why I loathe the bloke ... he thinks he has power and control over anything that happens here. When in reality, Niles and the owners of RFC are the ones calling the shots. Darnot couldn't throw me out of here even if he wanted to.

"When I tell Niles Harrington about your latest stunt, as well as the speeding incident you narrowly escaped an arrest from in London, he's going to send you packing. All of us here in the organization have tried for years to curb your reckless behavior. And even though you might be the most talented thing to fall into England's lap since Killian Ramsey, you're still a liability. A careless prat who'd rather spend time playing pranks than winning matches. Aren't you sick of it, yet, Jude? Don't you want to grow up? Take care of your brothers?"

This has me standing and slapping my palms down on his priceless antique desk. "Don't you dare say a word about my brothers."

I wish I could punch the satisfied smirk right off his lips. "Didn't think we knew about London, huh? And with an employee of the academy in the car, no less."

I falter, my heart stuttering to a halt. "She had nothing to do with my actions. She was only along as my assistant, there is a contract to prove it."

"And though that may be, her position here is still in jeopardy."

God fucking dammit, he was goading me. Pressing a thumb into a bullet wound and twisting it around.

None of this would matter if I didn't actually … fancy the girl. How stupid am I? My mission has been to shag her into next Tuesday, and now it was going on more than a month of me chasing her around and I've only just kissed her not more than fifteen minutes ago.

And here I am, sitting in Darnot's office, talking about the future of her job instead of snogging her senseless in our secret tunnel.

Bloody hell, the taste of her. I am the kind of prick who is used to thinking about the next woman I'd fuck as I was fucking the current one. I've been spoiled with the riches of the most gorgeous females in the land, and it is a fact that if you have too much of anything, you'll grow bored with it.

So what is it about Aria Lloyd that is keeping my skittish attention?

Why am I instantly drawn to her?

Indeed, exactly like with every girl before her, I am attracted in a wholly male, animalistic way.

To her rounded ass, the plump lips in a cherry hue, all the velvety, cream-colored skin. The way her long sheets of sunlight-colored hair fall down her back, and how innocent she comes off when I know, deep down, she is really as cynical as the rest of us.

But what my dodgy brain leaves out of it, what it deceives from me until I am already in too deep, is that we are more alike than I ever initially realized.

For months, she's been eating lunch in *my* spot, the one I've run to since I was a child at the academy when I just needed to turn the world off. I hid down there for almost forty-eight hours after my parents were killed.

Aria is the breadwinner of her family, the one who makes sure it stays afloat and no one is left behind. Exactly the same kind of responsibilities and pressure I put on my own shoulders.

And there is an indescribable bond that joins us, one I can only quantify by saying that I see the twinkle of it each time I look in her eyes. Maybe it's our pain that draws us toward each other like magnets, at losing parents or possibly losing one. Maybe it is something else, of that I'm not sure.

All I know is that it is there, and I am not going to let her be taken down with me since I'm the one that fucked up for the umpteenth time.

"It will never happen again. You have my word. From now

until the time that I get promoted to the first squad, I'll do nothing but eat, sleep, play football, and act like an altar boy."

I'm begging, about to kiss this deplorable man's shoes, but I don't care at this point.

Darnot's nose lifts superiorly into the air. "Your word doesn't mean shite. But I'll tell you what does. Cock up again and you'll not only be thrown out of the academy but I'll terminate your girlfriend, too. And blackball her from getting any position here in Clavering."

He's dropped the guillotine. Going forward, if I step out of line even a fraction, Aria is going to burn with me.

I can't let that happen.

17

ARIA

It's a rare day when Dad is feeling well enough to venture outside, much less a location where people are congregating.

But today, this Saturday, he woke up bright as a daisy and asked to walk up the road to watch the Rogue Academy game.

Most weekend days, there is a game at the academy. Between the younger squads, the mid-level blokes and players like Jude who are on the cusp of being international superstars, there is always someone playing in the small stadium housed on Rogue's campus.

"You're sure you feel up to this?" I hover next to him as we walk, ready at any moment to catch him.

Dad smiles, sniffing the air and snuggling down into his beige jacket. "Would you stop worrying your beautiful head about me? I'm fine. It feels nice to take a stroll outside."

Watching him smile makes a small grin pop onto my lips as well, but I'll never stop worrying. He's too thin, has lost practically a third of his body weight since he was diagnosed. The skin around his eyes is grey and drooping, and I made him wear two hats to cover his vulnerable, bald scalp.

"Who is playing today, anyway?" I ask, trying to go along with this charade that he is healthy and this is normal.

"The advanced players, the ones about to be called up to London." Dad claps. "One thing about living in Clavering; you can say that you watched some football legend play before he ever made his premier league debut."

My mind instantly goes to Jude. It isn't a matter of if he'd become the next football icon for England; it is when. The hourglass is rapidly losing sand ... it could be any day.

And what I would do, then?

Blimey, what a daft question. I'll do nothing. Because ... Jude means nothing to me. And I mean nothing to him. That much was clear after he kissed me in the tunnel, left abruptly, and never got back in touch. That had been more than seventy-two hours ago, and though my pride and foolish heart are wounded, I'll never tell a soul that.

It doesn't matter that I am going to see him play, or at least I can convince myself of that by the time we take our seats near the opposing keeper's net. Dad is feeling well enough for an afternoon of football, and that is the only reason I am going to sit in the Rogue stadium.

There is no other reason than that.

Okay, *fine*, maybe I wanted a reason to look at Jude without him being able to look at me. Crucify me for wanting to stare at the guy who kissed my knickers off the other day and hasn't spoken to me since.

"You're comfortable?" I place a blanket around Dad's shoulders and make sure we both have an empty seat next to us.

Even though these matches feature players who will someday make it big, the town of Clavering and the residents within it have grown tired of them. Something is only exciting when you can't have it much, and with the academy matches, the townspeople can have them all the time.

Come to think of it, that's a great analogy about Jude's fascination with me.

"Love, I'm just peachy." He grins and pats the seat next to him for me to sit down.

I do, and immediately spot the boy, the one who's been driving me stark raving mad, running around the pitch.

I've seen Jude practice before, have even seen him on television in some of the youth national team matches if my dad happened to have them on. But seeing him play right before my eyes? It's ... magical.

Jude Davies was made to gallivant around the pitch, leaving opponents in his wake. His body and movement are fluid as if gravity and the laws of physics do not apply to him. The way he juggles the ball, passing it through his teammates' feet and past walls of defenders ... Jude makes this look as easy as breathing. When in reality, I wouldn't be able to accomplish that blindfolded with a gun to my head.

Watching him play is like glimpsing a solar eclipse; you realize this kind of talent only comes around every so often and you better risk the damage to your eyesight to see it.

"Blimey, that boy can play," Dad whispers; just the act of viewing Jude on the field is akin to a religious experience.

I nod, not really talking to him, or anyone. "Yes, he can."

The match is a complete blowout, with the other academy scoring no goals by the time the referee blows the final whistle. Dad cheers and claps along with the sparse crowd, and people begin to filter out of the small stadium.

When I look up from grabbing the small bag of supplies I brought with us in case Dad needed something, the one person I had been hoping to fully avoid is walking straight to us.

I wore a cap to hide my face, and Jude has never seen my father, so I'm confused about how he spots us so quickly. Or maybe he knew I'd been here the entire game ... it would explain the *four* goals he scored. I mean … if I was even motivation for him.

"Aria, I didn't know you'd be coming to this game." Jude's eyes fixate on me the minute he comes to the barrier of the stands.

Dad and I stand about four rows up, and one of the two security guards tasked with keeping this match civil is looking this way from the other end of the pitch.

My father eyes me as well, and when I look up at him, the irises that match my own are wide and curious. "You two know each other?"

I shrug, trying to play it nonchalantly. "We've bumped into each other on campus …"

As if it's not a big deal that I haven't mentioned I'm friends, or kissing mates, with the most famous English football prodigy in, well, history.

"Sir, it's very nice to meet you." Jude sticks out his hand for my dad to shake.

Dad takes it, stunned. "And you, as well. Hell of a match."

Jude shrugs. "Eh, it was a friendly. We'll have to get you two up to Wembley for a proper match."

I swear Dad might have just swallowed his tongue. "That … I would be honored."

"Consider it done." Jude smiles kindly at him. "Can I steal you for a minute?"

This question is directed at me, and my stomach leaps into my throat. "We really should be getting home …"

Dad nudges me. "I can manage to get out of the stadium myself, and don't argue with me, I'm only bloody walking. Promise there will be no cartwheels or one-legged races."

I roll my eyes at him, but he continues. "Talk for a minute. I'll just be right outside on the pavement waiting for you."

And though I know I shouldn't, I meet Jude down in the first row as he hops the barrier and takes a seat.

18

JUDE

Two days.

That's how long it's taken me to decide that I don't want to listen to anyone's bloody rules.

Forty-eight hours are how long it's taken me to realize that no matter the consequences that fall upon our heads, I want another taste of Aria.

In the time that I've laid my head down the past two nights, I've spent a majority of that pillow time thinking and deliberating what I should say to her. And knowing that she's probably miffed that I went radio silent after I ran out on her in the tunnel.

When she sits next to me, her elbows crossing over her chest and unintentionally trussing up those perfectly round tits, it's no mystery that she's angry.

"I need to get back out to my dad, so what can I do for you this time, Jude?"

Ignoring her ire, I flash her a cheeky grin. "Wanted to see me play, huh?"

She glares. "I came because my father felt healthy enough to want to attend a match."

I cringe for putting my foot in my mouth. "That was meant to make me feel like an arsehole, wasn't it?"

"You're not as daft as I thought," Aria mocks.

"And you're being cheeky because I didn't get in touch after I said I would."

She looks away as soon as I bring up the kiss in the tunnel, and now I *really* feel like a wanker. "You don't need to patronize me, Jude. I'm not one of your kit chasers, or an international model waiting to grope your crotch."

That has me swallowing a laugh because Aria has truly caustic humor but right now is not the time for a chuckle. "And I like you because of it."

"Or in spite of it. Part of me thinks you only chase me around like you do because I'm a bit more of a challenge."

"Give yourself some credit, you're loads more than a *bit* of a challenge. And so what if I do like it? Why does a man enjoying a hard to get woman always have to be some big deal? I play games for a living, Aria, so I find excitement in them in my personal life. Doesn't mean I won't also enjoy it *thoroughly* when I catch you."

A blush steals over her normally cream-colored cheeks. "Who says I'm going to let you?"

"Oh, let's stop playing *that* game. No more sense in lying about how we feel ... and no, I can't believe those words just came out of my mouth."

Aria looks up to the grey sky and laughs. "Is this a complete joke?"

"Huh?" I ask, confused.

She looks back down at me. "You're Jude Davies. Freaking football star of our generation. You date models and party in Ibiza, and I'm ... me. I have no time to kiss you in tunnels and yet all I can think about is that. And I'm not stupid enough to think that it meant a thing to you, but *my God*, don't sit here and lie to my face."

And now she has my heart softening. "First off, I only partied in Ibiza once and don't remember it. Which scares me and I'll never go back. Next, who cares who the bloody hell I am? I'm a man, a cocky, daft one usually. And yes, the kiss meant something, as much as it pains me to even talk about it. Because, no, I don't care that I admitted it to you, but damn it, I really would just rather kiss you and shut your overthinking brain up."

So that's exactly what I do.

Grabbing her face, I pull her mouth onto mine and prove to Aria that the chase is *so* worth it. I kiss the girl until we're breathless, until my lips chap from the cold and she's trying to press her tits, the ones I desperately want my hands on, into my pecs.

She breaks off, heaving in lungfuls of air, her whiskey-colored eyes intense on mine. "My dad ..."

Oh, right ... her father is waiting outside the stadium for her. "Yeah, shite ..."

But before I let her go, I've been mulling over an idea for those two days that I just decided would be a wonderful one.

"My mates and I, Kingston and Vance, you might have seen them around campus? Well, Vance grew up in Brighton near the beach, and we have a short international break that lines up with classes being postponed. It's in a week. Why don't you come with us?"

Aria bristles. "As what? Your assistant? Or part of the posse of models you seem to travel with? Either way, the answer is no."

My hands shoot out, ready to argue my point when Aria cuts me off before I can utter a word.

"Jude, I barely did anything last time. I can't justify you paying me to sit around at matches and in hotel suites just because you have money to throw away and want a good laugh."

I'm invading her space in two seconds flat. "I don't want you to come along as my handler, Aria. Or even my assistant. I want you to come along as a girl I'm interested in."

What is it about this girl that keeps pushing my buttons? For my sake, I should leave her alone. She bothers me in the best way possible, and right now, I can't take that risk.

But, I should really leave her alone for *her* sake. Headmaster Darnot knows about London and the speeding incident and has threatened to issue her walking papers.

And yet ... there that rush of carnal adrenaline comes. The one that wants to corrupt her, to show her what my world is like, to pull her down into the madness.

Aria's blond hair whips in the wind, and I realize she might be cold. I can play in almost any condition, my skin having developed an extra layer with all these years on the pitch. But the most surprising realization that hits me is that, if I was wearing one, I'd offer her my coat.

"Even if that's the truth, I can't leave my dad."

"I'll have a nurse come in and check on him," I offer immediately.

Those hazel eyes, flecked with streaks of gold gleaming in the brisk sunlight, tell me she'll never go for it. "You know I won't let you do that."

"Yes, I know, but it was worth a shot." I sulk.

"I just ... I can't leave him. He's almost done with this round of chemo and it's been brutal. But ... I don't want you to stop."

"Stop what?"

"Chasing me." Aria gives me a small smile.

And as we part, me hopping the barrier and her heading up the concrete steps to join her dad; I promise myself, and her, that I won't.

19

ARIA

"So, Jude Davies, huh?"

Welp, I should have known this was coming from the moment the academy's football star approached us in the stands.

Dad sits in his recliner as I make dinner, chicken pot pie, the nightly news on in the background.

"What about him?" I answer, purposely turning to the stove so he can't see my face.

Dad chuckles in the background. "I may be sick, love, but I'm not blind. The boy fancies you, and I'd say the feeling is mutual."

"I'm glad you think you can read minds now. Is that a side effect of the treatments?" My response is cheeky.

"Aria, don't avoid the subject." He laughs.

I sigh, lining the pie tins with the pre-made crust I bought from the supermarket. When I've poured the mixture and set the timer for the oven, I place them inside and wander into the living room.

Sitting down on the sofa, I watch idly as the news anchor

talks about the current currency calculations of the British pound.

"We've known each other for about two months. Honestly, at first, I told him to piss off. What I know of him is the stuff of tabloid legend and football fame … neither of which I have time for. But, as these kinds of boys usually do, he wore me down."

"He was nothing but cordial at the stadium," my father points out.

I raise an eyebrow at him. "He was trying to impress you."

"Which is the sign that a boy likes your daughter. If he wasn't interested in you in a real way, he wouldn't have been bothered to meet me. That makes most men sound like scoundrels, but I know these things … I'm a former scoundrel." Dad smiles proudly at me.

I pat his arm gently. "You're too nice in your opinion of Jude … but yes, I'm starting to realize, unfortunately, his intentions might be genuine."

"So, what is the problem, then?" Dad knows I'm not saying something.

When you grow up, as a female, with only your male parent as the voice of reason, reliability, knowledge, and everything else … there are some topics that get left off the table. Dating is one of them. I remember, when I broke up with my secondary school boyfriend, my dad was sick at the time but still trying to mask that he wasn't scared out of his mind. He tried to talk to me about how I was feeling, and I shut myself in my room for three days, had a good cry, and told him never to mention it again.

Having him talk to me about Jude, when we've avoided the topic of my love life for so long, feels strange. But, I don't really have any other friends, and I can't tell Patricia and Louisa I'm flirting with an academy player, least of all Jude Davies, so I guess Dad it is.

"We come from massively different worlds. He has the universe on a string, and I live in the dumps of Clavering. Not to mention, I have to be here to help take care of—"

Dad cuts me off. "If you blame not dating the next superstar of the Rogue Football Club on me, I'll throw this pot pie you just worked so hard on at the wall. Do you know how fast I'd give away your hand if Jude Davies asked?"

I know he's only joking, but I'm not in the mood for sarcasm. "Har, har. Seriously, Dad, I have other things to worry about. And I'm not the type of girl to take charity from some footballer pretending to be my white knight. Lord knows if I give him that power, he'll just abuse it."

Dad holds his hands up. "I don't want to venture into that territory."

My face breaks out in embarrassed flames. "Blimey, that's not what I meant! All I am trying to say is I crave independence and don't want anyone else telling me how to live if I allow them to get to know me. Plus, the whole he's an international playboy thing. I just ... why me?"

Now he sighs. "I thought I built up your confidence sturdier than this over the years, surely. But I'll tell you again so you hear me. Aria, you are one of the strongest, most intelligent, genuinely beautiful people inside and out that I've ever met. And that's coming from someone who raised you, so I know I did a good job. Honestly, you remind me a lot of your mother."

This is the first time he's ever said that. "Which means that I'm predisposed to run away from someone I have feelings for."

"You're like her in the fact that you want more out of life. That you're fiercely self-sufficient and don't often ask for help. That your spirit carries you through tough times. But besides that, you're all me, kiddo. You stay when the going gets tough, and that's what counts. You have a heart wider than the English Channel, and you can identify those who mirror your kind of compassion. It's why you're interested in Jude; you can recognize that he is someone to take a chance on."

His answer gives me pause, and I walk to the kitchen to decompress. After pulling the pot pie out of the oven and setting the table, I grab myself a rare glass of wine and put a glass of water out of for my dad. Dad turns off the TV and joins me at our small kitchen table, the one with a wobbly leg with a permanent book under it.

"He invited me to go to Brighton next weekend."

"That will be fun, I love the beach, and the pier is neat." Dad tucks into his pot pie and groans with satisfaction. "This is delicious, Aria."

I take a bite of my own and commend myself for how good I'm getting at cooking meals. "Thank you. I told Jude I can't go."

Dad sets his fork down with a clatter. "Why would you do that?"

"For all the reasons we just talked about."

"Aria, please go. You will never regret taking a chance on this boy, or this trip. It's time that you stopped allowing me to chain you to this town. It's time for you to spread your wings and experience what the rest of the world has to offer. You live just under two hours from Brighton, a brilliant little beach town, and you've never been. You're going. I said so, and it's final."

No matter how much I argue with him, he'll find a way to make me go with Jude next weekend. So for the first time in my life, I let someone tell me what to do, and just settle with that decision.

20

ARIA

After finding Jude the day after the talk with my dad, I told him I'd be open to traveling to Brighton with him and his friends.

That earned me a salacious make-out session, one I was thankful we were in the tunnel for, and a pump of his fist that I'd actually agreed to go with him.

So now here I sit, in the back of a stretch Hummer limo with three strapping blokes, one of whom is currently trying to make me sit in his lap.

"Jude, stop it," I hiss, swatting his hands away.

He shrugs those massive shoulders, trying to look innocent. "My mates don't care, they've seen worse."

Arching a brow, I look down the limo at Kingston and Vance. "And this is supposed to make me feel better?"

"That did sound pretty daft, mate." Vance nods in agreement with me.

Kingston just looks confused, as if my refusal to sit in Jude's lap is some weird gesture he's never seen before. "I'm confused."

"I can tell." I chuckle.

"He's just never seen a girl with a backbone before, it's nothing personal." Jude grins.

"Glad I can teach them, and you, what a real lady acts like." Reaching into my bag, I pluck my headphones out and plug them into my phone, flipping through my music library after they've sealed me off from the world.

Jude slings his arm around my shoulders and pulls me into his side, which I guess is his consolation for me refusing to bounce on his lap the entire two-hour ride to Brighton. The sounds of Coldplay fill my ears, and I'm just about to close my eyes and nod into my first relaxing moment of the last year, when Kingston's voice shouts over my music.

"So, Aria, tell me how to find a girl who'll keep me on my toes like you keep Jude on his."

Vance shakes his head at his friend because he probably assumes this attempt at learning something will be hopeless.

I pull out my right earbud, squaring my shoulders for the conversation we're about to have.

"Are you ready to settle down with a girlfriend?" I pose the most obvious question.

Kingston's pretty-boy face screws up in disgust. "Bloody hell, no!"

"Then you're not ready for a girl like me." I smile meanly.

"So, she's your girlfriend, Jude?" Vance asks from his seat at the front of the limo, right by the partition that the driver rolled up.

My heart seizes, and everyone in the car is holding their breath waiting for Jude to answer.

"You're going to put me on the spot like that?" Jude looks like he might leap across the leather seats and strangle Vance.

"Come on, superstar." Vance wiggles his eyebrows at him.

My hands begin to sweat as I chant over and over in my head, *please don't embarrass me, please don't embarrass me*.

Jude clears his throat. "I fancy Aria, a lot. And I like spending time with her. The reason I invited her on this trip is to see where we can go. If you want to call that a girlfriend, then sure, she's my girlfriend."

Blowing out the breath I'm holding, a grin spreads across my lips. Because that was the exact right answer, the one I didn't even realize I needed Jude to give.

Sure, we have been flirting and trying to sneak around to see each other. He's met my father and knows a part of me, my singing, that no one else is privy to. But we need to spend more time together. I need to decide if my doubts about him outweigh the pull my heart and mind feel whenever I think about him.

"I'll decide if and when I want to claim that title." I cross my arms with a smug grin.

The limo zooms down the motorway, and I get lost in my music once more. When it begins to slow about an hour and a half later, I turn to look out the windows, discovering we've arrived in Brighton.

The town of Brighton is unique and charming, with shops along a main road, restaurants facing the water, a pier with old-school carnival games, and from what Jude says, a happening nightlife scene. The minute we arrive in Vance's hometown, we're driven to his parents' house. Or, the house that Vance helped purchase for them with money from the contract he signed last year.

It's a modern, glass and steel thing right on the water, and honestly, it's not my style at all. To me, it looks like a museum; I prefer the homey, English feel of a local pub, or furniture passed down from your grandmother. But, it's a long way from my musty row home, and the room his mum shows me to has its own tub, so I'm not going to utter a word of complaint.

"Ready to go?" Jude stops in my doorway twenty minutes after I've set my bags down on the bed.

"What? Go where?" I'm surprised we're moving again so quickly.

"Time to go out. When we have a few days off, we like to let our hair down. And that means lots of alcohol and shenanigans."

Why do I feel like this bloke and his mates are about to get me into serious trouble? And why do I like the thought of that?

"Give me a few minutes to get dressed. Are we going somewhere posh?" Not that I had clothes nearly as expensive to measure up to the likes of Jude, Kingston, and Vance.

"Jeans and a nice top will do. I can help you pick them out, if you'd like." His green eyes dance with sexual energy.

Something inside my belly flips, and I know we're on the precipice of falling into an act we can't take back. It both surprises me and scares me that I'm excited for it, that the anticipation only adds to the heat building between us.

I shut the door on him for good measure, because if he asks again, I'll be tempted to let him do more than select my outfit.

Twenty minutes later and we're out the door again, my threadbare black jeans and the most expensive top I own, a thirty-pound maroon blouse from H&M, looking completely average next to the demigods in their designer clothes. I try to push it out of my mind and focus on the fact that I'm in a new place with no responsibilities ... at least for the weekend.

The pier in Brighton is adorable, and the pebble-covered beach is vastly different than the only other sand I've felt. When I was seven, my parents took me to Greece to summer and from what I can remember, it was the most magical time I've ever had.

But living in Clavering, and never really getting to escape to the coast since my mother left us, I don't often see the beach or the ocean.

We start the night at a neat Mexican restaurant, with a lounge feel and windows overlooking the ocean.

"A round of tequila shots for the table, and then you can keep the margarita pitchers coming," Kingston instructs the waitress.

"Oh, I'm fine, thanks, just water," I beg off.

All three men eye me skeptically, but Vance is the one who speaks. "You're legal, right?"

"Of course." My pride is wounded. I'm only one year younger than them.

"So, have a drink. We have a car service, you're on vacation, who cares?" Vance presents me with the situation.

Jude, who is sitting next to me at the four-person high-top, rubs my jean-clad thigh under the table. "Whatever you choose, I'm going to take care of you tonight."

His words are meant to soothe, but they only cause a furious simmer to bubble right at the apex of my core. His big hand on my leg, the presence of three alpha males, his words about taking care of me ...

If I didn't have the attention of all three, I would have fanned my face right about now.

"Okay, I'll have a drink."

In the end, I do the shot with them and have one margarita. It's been so long since I had liquor, that the drinks go straight to my head. The buzz stays there long after we've inhaled guacamole, fajitas, tacos, and plantains. After dinner, the four of us move to a nightclub, Jude lacing his fingers through mine as we push through the surging crowd. The place is loud and electric, and when he presses his body to mine and begins to sway our hips in time, I become feverish.

My arms wind backward, around his neck, as I lose myself in the music. It's a techno beat set to a Rihanna song, one perfect for this kind of atmosphere. It pulses with the crowd, and though I've always loved music for the voices in it and how it makes me feel emotionally ... right now, I'm loving that it's invading the part of me that needs to move my body.

Jude surrounds me, his long limbs enveloping me, and an unmistakable hardness presses against my backside. When I feel his lips press down on the sensitive spot halfway between my ear and collarbone, I jump, goose bumps breaking loose on my flesh.

"I need some air," I shout over the noise and point to the exit.

Because I do, and I also need one more quiet moment to consider what I'm about to allow myself to drown in.

My physical, and mental, attraction to Jude.

The sounds of the nightclub begin to fade away as I tipsily stumble out of it, the beer I consumed half an hour ago only adding to the nice hum the drinks created in my system. Instead of booming music and the shouts of people, waves crashing against the beach fill my ears, and I walk toward them.

Jude catches up to me as I sit myself in a red and white striped chair to watch the ocean lap the stones. It gives me a sense of peace I haven't felt in a very long time.

"Too much for you back there?" he asks as he takes the chair next to me.

I press a hand to my rapidly beating chest. "Not at first, but after a while, I need a break."

"Sounds a lot like what I'm always thinking," Jude murmurs, and I turn to look at him.

His eyes aren't on me but gazing out at the dark line of the horizon, where the murky black water meets the starry sky. A bead of sweat trickles down from his temple to his jaw, and I find myself desperate to lay my tongue along that path. It's a strange notion because even with my ex-boyfriend, I never felt the kind of physical pull I do when my eyes hold Jude in them. His dark hair is tousled, wild, and he makes my mouth go dry just studying his profile.

"Is it too much for you? All of this?" I ask, repositioning to lean on my side so that I can face him.

Jude turns to me and doesn't touch me but we're close enough that I can feel his heat. "Yes, and no. I was born for this life, brought up in it. Really, it's all I've ever known. I thrive on the attention, the cheers, the boos. My energy builds from the circus of it all, and yet, sometimes, I just want to shut myself up in my room and never come out. I am their prince and their scapegoat. When I'm winning for them, I am untouchable, sitting at the top of the world. And when I cock up, they're the first to start digging my grave and throwing me six feet under. It's a lot of pressure. Admitting that probably makes me a wanker, but I have a feeling you won't spill my secret."

I get this gnawing feeling that not a lot of people see this side of Jude Davies, if any. It makes me, in turn, feel vulnerable and I'm nervous with the thought that he's trusting me with his deepest emotions.

"But you have to know that this is what you were meant to do, right? You have more talent in your pinky than most do in their entire bodies."

Jude's face grows dark as he nods. "And what about you?"

I snort out a laugh; the beer making my defenses come down. "What about me? A seamstress for a football club? Oh, and you forgot to add nighttime janitor."

Jude bridges the gap between us, taking a lock of my hair in his hands and rubbing it back and forth as he talks.

"Don't do that. Don't act as if you don't have the singing voice of a bloody angel. You sound better than anyone I've ever heard on the radio, Aria, and you're doing nothing with it."

Wrenching out of his grasp, fury lights my lowered inhibitions on fire. "You have no idea what you're talking about."

"I know you're working a dead-end job when you could be providing for your family with the ease of posting a video on

YouTube. I might not know much about the recording industry, but I have a feeling you'd be signed in three seconds flat if someone discovered you. You're wasting time!"

Jude stands, marching down the beach. Is this how it will be with us? This push and pull? The ferocity of emotion and attraction waging war against each other.

I follow him, trying to calm myself down enough to tell him my biggest secret. When I reach him, I tug on his elbow; the moonlight bending around his body as he turns to face me.

I've never told anyone, not even my dad, what I am about to reveal to Jude.

"When I was ten, I joined the chorus at my school. I loved it, fell in love with singing right away. The choir director told me I had a real talent and wanted me to start voice lessons on the side. I'd already been a music addict since the first day my dad had played a Nina Simone CD on our living room stereo when I was five. So I went home, professed my love for it, and asked my mom if she could sign me up for lessons. By that point in their marriage, and in my life, my mom was distant. She worked all the time, acted as if every word I uttered was a nuisance, and just generally didn't want to be around me. I remember it so clearly; my mom looked me in the eye, told me I was a foolish girl to think I could become a singer, and that it was a useless career path. She told me my voice was average, and a week later, she'd packed her things and walked out the door."

In front of my very eyes, Jude transforms into the very definition of empathy and fury, all at the same time.

"What a bloody *cunt*." It comes off his lips like the worst kind of curse.

The word is foul but accurate. All I can do is shrug in the directness of his gaze. I expect him to say more, but Jude only looks at me, assessing, searching. A few moments after I confess about the most shameful moment of my life, he finally speaks.

"We should get back to the club, find Kingston and Vance. It's getting late."

21

JUDE

I've been a gentleman or as much of one as I could possibly be, the entire night. And now I am tired of that.

Creeping across the hall, I come to stand in front of the door to the bedroom Aria is staying in. I'm not sure what Vance told his mum and dad about our situation, but it either wasn't enough or was too much so that they'd put us in separate rooms.

As if that was going to keep me from getting into her bed.

It's the first time, aside from the hotel room, that I am in close proximity to Aria, at night, in a bedroom. We finally wrangled Kingston and Vance from the club to go home around two a.m. One had his tongue down a girl's throat, you can only guess that was Mr. Phillips, and the other had been having a stare off with some bird across the room. Vance claims it was nothing, that she was an old acquaintance, but I'd have to question him about it later as there seemed to be daggers floating between their two glares.

When we finally arrived back to the Morley residence, Aria bid me a good night in an awkward, forced parting gesture. She side-hugged me and then scurried off to her room like a frightened mouse. She was still rattled by the conversation we had on the beach, I know it. It was deep, far too heavy than either of us had intended for this trip to be.

Too bad I'm not more honorable, or that would have given me pause. The scoundrel in me takes no caution, however, as I bypass knocking and simply, quietly let myself into her bedroom.

Aria hadn't locked the door, and I twist that into a signal that she wants me to pay her a late-night visit. I am about to show her just how interested in her I am, in the best way I know how.

As I inch closer to the bed, wearing nothing but the boxer briefs I typically sleep in, my heart begins to thump. Out of anticipation, but also out of nervousness. What if she kicks me in the bollocks and sends me packing?

"Jude."

Aria's quiet voice fills the air of the dark room, and now I know that she watched me enter, cross the floor, and come to stand next to her bed. She's been awake the entire time.

I kneel next to where she lies on the outermost spot of the queen bed, her body obscured by the duvet. From the scant amount of moonlight filtering through the drapes, I can make out her elegant cheekbones and the way her wheat-blond hair splays over the pillow.

"You have more talent in your pinky than most people have in their entire bodies," I repeat her own words back to her. "Everything you do matters to me."

They are simple thoughts, but I hope they get a clear message across to Aria. Since the moment she caught me in the locker room, there has been this unexplainable urge to learn everything about her. From the way she looks while angry, or sad, or happy, to her biggest dreams and the way she sounds as she's being kissed.

I'm not able to make out the look in her eye after I say these words to her, but it doesn't matter. Because one second I'm kneeling there, and the next, Aria is throwing herself at me, no other noises ripple in the room aside from our lips bridging the gap between us.

She half-pulls me, and I help the rest of the way by climbing, on top of her. My body fits into the groove of hers with only the duvet between us, and her hands begin to explore every naked part of my skin.

Those tiny hands skim the length of my back and in an instant, I'm so bloody hard for her that my balls ache something bad. Her fingertips tickle my sides as they peruse as my tongue invades her mouth, fucking it like I wish to fuck her.

Aria is squirming beneath me and the sheets, and in one smooth pull, I'm under them with her. From what I can feel, her pajamas are a set of cotton pants and short-sleeved button-up. It doesn't surprise me that her choice of sleepwear is conservative; if anything, it fuels my desire more. She is both innocent and willingly giving herself to a wolf in wolf's clothing.

I am no gentleman, as I said. Once Aria allows me full access to her naked body, I'm not going to slow down.

"Do you want me?" I tear my mouth from hers.

Aria's breathing is husky, jagged. I can feel the indecision on her tongue; sense it in her body language.

"You have to answer me. It's the only time I'll ask because once we start, I won't be able to stop. So, tell me to stop."

With all the other girls, sex has been a release. I am a physical man, with a body I work hard for and have built for exerting energy. I can't be expected to play football all hours of the day, and sex is the next best enjoyable thing. I never cared who they were, how well they conversed. It didn't bother me that I had no clue where they came from or what their family was like or what they did for a living.

Being with Aria, though? There is this indescribable knowing that shakes me down deep. I care about all of it.

It would be better than even football, of that I am afraid. When I finally touch her skin, feel her come alive under my fingertips, I know I'll think of nothing else but the distance between my lips and hers. Between my cock plunging into her. Each time she sighs, I feel like I want to live in that sound forever.

It's cliché to say I have never felt this way, but it is true. I have never felt the maddening desire to repeat this moment over and over again. And nothing has even happened yet.

Nothing has ever been as addicting as she is.

"Stop," she says quietly, and something inside me dies.

Probably the raging blue bollocks offing themselves, knowing they won't be getting a release tonight.

"I shouldn't have asked," I grumble, my head dropping to the pillow, next to her head.

"Sorry ..." Aria murmurs.

This has me tensing. Pulling my chin, up, I palm her face. "Look at me. I did not mean it in that way. I won't rush you, but once you tell me you're ready, there will be no holding back. Of course, my cock is disappointed, but that doesn't mean *I'm* disappointed. You should feel explicitly comfortable whenever you decide to—"

"Jude, I'm not a virgin," she exclaims.

My randy knob perks up at the word virgin. The *bastard*. "Oh."

It's the daftest thing I could have possibly said, but she kind of shocked me, and now I roll over to face the ceiling and contemplate how heroic I was trying to be by saving her virginity from my corrupting ways.

Aria clears her throat. "I had a boyfriend in secondary school before my dad got sick. We were pretty serious, or serious enough that I'd thought, naively, we'd be together forever. But ... I respect you for trying to honor my virtue."

Only this girl could make me crack up laughing at a time like this. "I was trying hard, wasn't I?"

Her head rustles on the bed as she nods. "You were. And … it's not that I don't want to. Truly, I do. It's just … I reserve sex as something special. I'm not ready for all the weight that comes with it. I hope you understand."

"I'm not a caveman, love. Of course, I understand."

"Well, you never know with you, Davies." Aria snickers.

Pulling her to me, I nuzzle my nose in her hair playfully. Me, Jude Davies, being playful with a girl. Are pigs flying over the house?

"Yes, you can stay," she answers the question I didn't even ask.

So, for the first time in a *very* long time, I snuggle up to a woman and fall asleep, no funny business about it.

22

ARIA

When you're young, say nineteen, the attention and lust that a boy directs toward you is all-encompassing as it is. But add a personality like Jude Davies, and it's a wonder I can even think about anything else.

Our relationship is blinding and intense, inking out every other aspect of my life if I am within a twenty-foot radius of Jude. He leaves notes on my sew house station, telling me to meet him in the tunnels at a certain time. Or he shows up in a different location each night of the week during my janitorial shift to distract me into taking off my shirt ... or something more scandalous.

I've never been so brazen. It feels taboo and ... almost illegal. Which only makes me want to do it that much more.

And the time we do spend together that is planned ... I never want it to end. Being close to him gets my heart racing and leaves me in a trance.

Ever since the night we slept, just slept, together at Vance's parent's house, it's been a whirlwind. Every spare second I have to give goes to Jude. When he's not practicing or doing the seven hundred other activities that go into becoming the most incredible football player in the world, he's with me. We communicate constantly, and it all happened like the flick of a light switch.

One minute, my world was work and trying to save my dad's life. And the next, I'd condensed what little room I had left, packed it up and gave it to the boy I've been dangerously attracted to from the day I laid eyes on him. Which was naked, in the locker room.

We still haven't had sex, but from the way he explored my body in the locker room the other night, I know we aren't far from it. He might have put his hands all over my breasts, and *blimey*, did he know how to use them.

I am afraid to do much more than that and rounding third base with our mouths or fingers is included. Not because I don't want to have sex with Jude, I *very* badly do.

But I know that, just like he said, once we start, we won't be able to stop. For me, when it comes to Jude, it is all or nothing. Something in the back of my mind recognized that the minute we took our clothes off in front of each other, it is going to be all the way or nothing at all.

This week, though, Jude is in Italy for a friendly match that the RFC first team is playing against the Rome club team. He's already been gone for two days, and I am watching the match this morning on the tiny TV Patricia keeps in the sew house.

"Look at the chap run." Patricia shakes her head appreciatively as Jude darts across the screen.

Due to good behavior, or so Jude told me, Niles Harrington decided to start him in today's match. I am so happy for him, as I know he's been down on himself lately for his lack of playing time in the premier league. In the back of my brain, however, I know that if he does well today and manages to keep his off-the-pitch antics to a minimum, it will only be a matter of time until he is called to London for good.

Louisa nods emphatically. "He has some legs on him."

Patricia, her old brows wrinkling, shoots her an annoyed glance. "That is not what I meant. I meant that being witness to that much talent ... a player like Jude Davies only comes around once a lifetime if you're a lucky supporter."

I keep my mouth shut, not wanting to sway one way or the other. The two ladies I work with have no idea that Jude is my boyfriend.

Am I allowed to call him that yet? I was the one who said I'd decide if and when we had those titles, and bloody hell, it's probably time. As much as my doubtful heart wanted to resist, and as much as I fought it tooth and nail to the point before that switch flipped, the reality is, I want Jude in my life.

The reality is, I am falling in love with a boy who threatened to take my heart and keep it forever. And I am willingly letting it happen.

"She's right," I pipe up, unable to help myself. "He's going to be the best player this generation has ever seen."

My eyes and hands stay focused on my work, but I can feel Louisa looking at me. "When did your tune on golden boy change?"

I shrug. "Who said it has? I just ... he seems to work hard."

It's a lame excuse, and I can feel both of them staring at me now.

"Do you have the flu?" Patricia asks, her expression one of utter confusion.

"Can we just get back to work?" I huff.

"There she is! The slave driver at her finest." Louisa wipes pretend sweat from her brow. "I was getting nervous there for a second."

So was I, as sweat trickles down the length of my spine. Jude and I might have unofficially given ourselves the title of boyfriend and girlfriend, but we haven't discussed the logistics of our relationship.

Can we be seen in public together?

Does the academy need to know?

Will we have to hide until I leave my job or he's promoted to the first team?

Even then, what would the papers say about us?

These are all questions I should probably ask Jude but don't have the courage to. Being together, it is so fresh and new ... this is the time where we are supposed to enjoy the honeymoon of it all without getting so bogged down in the questions and heaviness of life.

Unfortunately, when you're dating someone like Jude, that luxury doesn't seem to exist.

23

JUDE

If ice baths aren't already included in Dante's seven levels of hell, they should be.

At this point, my bollocks are probably shriveled up to the size of prunes, and I've lost the feeling in my toes so long ago, I'm not exactly sure they are still there. But, it is true when they say soaking your naked body in a tub of half-frozen water helps it recover more quickly. And with the brutal practices Gerard has been putting us through, and the rumor that I'll get to play with the first team next week, *finally*, I need to use every trick in the book.

My phone begins to ring on the table next to me, and I glance over to see it's an unlisted number.

Bloody hell.

"Hello?" I pick it up and rage begins to bubble through my veins.

"Mr. Davies, thanks for taking my call," a strange voice says on the other end.

"Who is this and how did you get this number?" I growl, annoyed that I've got another leak on my hands.

Five times ... it's happened five times where a paparazzo or mental fan has gotten my phone number and called it like mad. I've had to change it, block people, make sure I'm unlisted and even then there is this shite.

"No, no, I'm sorry, I should have introduced myself sooner. I'm Ian Rethal, we met at the open mic night in London? When your friend was on stage?"

A blurry memory comes back to me, because it was weeks ago, just after I first met Aria and asked her to accompany me to London. The pieces of my recall situate themselves in my mind, and I do remember the low level A&R guy coming up to me and asking about her.

"Yes, what can I do for you?" Now I listen, when I was two seconds away from hanging up and returning to the pain of the ice and the rest of the rugby match I had on.

"Sorry, it's taken me so long to get around to calling or reaching out to your friend. At first, I spelled her name wrong and couldn't find anything on social media. So I did some light detective work and traced her back to Rogue through her connection to you, but then I couldn't find any videos on YouTube or talent show mentions or ... well, anything about her singing."

My head shakes with annoyance. Not at him, or at Aria, but at the world. The reason he couldn't find anything online about Aria, or her incredible voice, is because she has no time for such things. The universe has thrown her a wicked punch by gifting her the tone of an angel, and the luck of the devil.

"No, you wouldn't be able to find her. She's off the grid, unfortunately."

"Yeah, kind of realized that. Anyway, I did snag a clip of her song at the open mic night, and it's taken a little bit of convincing for my bosses to want to lend me the budget, but I want to bring her in to record a demo."

This has me sitting up a little, the ice rattling around my frigid bones. "You do?"

In my mind's eye, I see Ian nodding on the other end. "Yep, and we'd like to bring her in right away. I haven't heard a voice like your friend Aria's in a long time ... it's a wonder she hasn't been picked up by a label, yet."

It's not a wonder, but I'm not going to tell a stranger the inner workings of her life. "Let me talk to her. In the meantime, can you email my manager your number and the label you work for? I'll give you his email, do you have a pen?"

I rattle off Barry's contact information as Ian tries to go through dates to record with me. But I shut him down, repeating that I need to connect with Aria first.

We hang up and I readjust in the tub, my teeth chattering together. Some of my teammates can remain in the ice baths for extended periods of time and be *comfortable* after the first few minutes. But me? It's always a struggle, no matter how often I immerse myself in this torture chamber, it never gets easier.

That's a feeling I'm not accustomed to. My entire life, I've been able to learn a skill and master it in a matter of a day or two. With each new technique on the football pitch, I've excelled at receiving the knowledge and being able to repeat it back perfectly. My talent, they say, was born with me ... but so was my ability to quickly pick up on things. Fame has been the same; I've learned the dark corners and lay of the land and chosen which way to point my feet. My party-boy attitude may land me in hot water at times, but at least I know the score.

Except ... with Aria, I can judge her mood and her actions about as well as I know which way the wind will turn. If I go to her with this news, will she be happy about it? Will she tell me to fuck off because she simply has no time to go somewhere to record a demo?

Or will she understand precisely how much this could

change her life? The times we've spoken about her singing, and the confession she made to me about her mother's reaction ... it's a touchy subject for her. I hope she knows that not only could a demo, and a record label hearing said demo, launch her music career and a dream she's yet to believe she can have, just my assumption, but ... this could mean serious money.

She's breaking her back working all these shifts at the academy. If one song or one album could net the kind of profits I think her voice is capable of, Aria could provide for herself and her father in ways she never thought possible.

As soon as I can walk properly after removing myself from this self-imposed tundra, I'll figure out exactly how to word it so that Aria will take this as an opportunity, and not just another burden to add to her plate.

When had I become the supportive guy who cares if the girl I am trying to sleep with follows her dreams or not? Before Aria, I rarely cared *if* those girls had dreams. Or a name.

Apparently, my feelings for her are just another part of Aria Lloyd that I can't quite grasp. But I am plunging full force ahead, even if the waters are bloody frigid.

24

JUDE

Sure enough, the following weekend, I'm asked to come to London and dress as a sub for the match.

Which means I won't be starting, but Niles is warming up to the idea that I can bring Rogue Football Club wins in spades.

It's a night game, and I arrive in London at nine a.m. with Aria snoozing softly on my shoulder as the driver of our town car pulls into the underground garage of the hotel. I convinced her, along with help from her dad after a sneakily placed phone call, that she could spare one night and come with me. After guilting her brilliantly to think I would lose the match if she wasn't present to watch me play, she finally relented.

She fell asleep with her headphones in on the drive, and I gently took them out and watched as she dreamed peacefully. I never noticed how the worry lines she always wore went away when she slept ... and wonder if it's the only time she feels at peace in her life.

I'm hoping I can make her this happy all the time.

With a few hours to kill before I have to be at the RFC facilities for pre-match strategy, warm-ups, and getting stretched by the massage therapist, I know just what I want to do with Aria.

"You've never been shopping in London. I figure it's time to get you a gift."

My girlfriend shifts uncomfortably next to me as we walk down the street. "I'm not sure about this. I don't need anything, and ... Jude, I don't want to spend your money."

I knew she'd say that. "Which is why I'll spend it for you. On you, rather. We're going out tonight and while you'd look bloody sexy in a paper bag, I want you to feel incredible. And don't give me that, 'expensive clothes are only a facade,' thing. I know they are. I'm not trying to make you fit in, but posh clothes make us feel posh ... that's all I'm trying to do."

Aria blinks up at me. "That was ... actually a very convincing argument."

"Good, I didn't feel like getting called a git at this moment."

Stopping in the middle of the pavement, I frame her face with my hands. Her sun-kissed hair floats on the wind, the silk of it tangling in my fingers as they dive into her scalp. Her round hazel eyes dance with a smile as I lean in, my lips on a very focused mission.

Aria's mouth bends to mine when I slip it over hers, the sweet sting of her vanilla citrus scent filling my nose. Is it a wonder I'm enraptured with this girl? The way she matches my kiss, melting into me as I lead us in the gentle rhythm of it.

The blood in my veins begins to boil, and if we weren't in public, I'd be tearing at her clothes right about now. That's the thing about our trysts ... we never have a place alone for them. It's a curse and a blessing; I can respect that Aria isn't ready for sex, and it makes it easier that we don't really have a place to do the dirty deed. But it also means that I am prone to humping her in barely concealed places.

Everything about her, from the dip of her waist to the blush that creeps over her cleavage when I nip at her neck. From the way she giggles at insignificant things, to the constant hum of her new favorite song she whistles throughout the day. Aria intrigues me in ways a woman never has.

I pull my lips from hers because if I don't I'll be mauling her in the street in two seconds and mirror the smile she's pressing to my mouth.

And since she's in such a good mood, it's probably time for me to broach the subject of recording a demo. It has been three days since I received the phone from Ian Rethal, and since we're in London, I've taken action without Aria's consent. Hopefully, she'll come around to my thrusting this news upon her.

"I meant to talk to you about something, love." I slip my hand into Aria's as we continue our walk down Bond Street.

There are probably people all over who will catch sight of me kissing, and strolling along with, an unknown female and begin to snap our picture, post them all over the Internet, and then the speculation will begin.

Who is she, where is she from, is she pretty or not, do they make a good couple?

Honestly, I don't care about any of it. I never have, and, especially haven't given a fuck about the public knowing that I'm actually dating someone. The only thing that concerns me is Aria's safety, and I'll do everything to protect her.

I'm good at that, protecting the people whom I love.

Wait ... did I just ... do I love Aria?

"Jude? You were about to talk to me about something?" she reminds me, snuggling into me as we pass posh shop after posh shop. "By the way ... should we be, um, walking like this?"

Her eyes flick to our conjoined hands, and I can feel the stares of those on the street starting to notice. We haven't discussed our press strategy or what we'd tell the headmaster or higher-ups in the academy if they found out we were dating.

Barry didn't even know yet, although he'd find out from Twitter in about five minutes if my calculations were correct.

Like most things in my life, I decide to wing it. Squeezing Aria's hand, I wink at her. "Who bloody cares, love? You're my girl, that's all they need to know. I'll deal with the flak from Headmaster Darnot, if there is any."

My answer is matter of fact, and we didn't need to dance around the subject any longer.

The blush that creeps across her delicate face is worth it. "So, back to you needing to tell me something ..."

A store, one I know has the reputation for designer clothes and expensive clients, pops up in our path. It's the kind of shop with girly, sparkly dresses in the window, and I duck us inside. Immediately, the ladies working the cash registers look up, and their mouths fall open. I feel Aria roll her eyes next to me, that's how accustomed I am getting to her, and I smirk my famous smirk while asking them to find the perfect dress that Aria could wear for our club outing tonight.

Kingston and Vance are coming in for the game, having no match at the academy today, and it has been too long since we caused some mischief.

While the shop ladies go to work and sit us down by the dressing room with glasses of champagne, Aria openly gapes at me.

"*Blimey*, your life is not even real." Her face scrunches up as the bubbles hit her nose after her first sip.

"Oh, it's real, love, and you're about to carve out a permanent path in it, too."

"What do you mean?" she asks.

I take a deep breath. "Someone from a record label saw your performance at the open mic night. He was sitting two tables away from me, noticed who I was and I suppose how intensely I was staring at you and asked for your name. His name is Ian

Rethal, he works for a big-time label here in London, and he loves your voice. Somehow, he tracked down my phone number and called me the other day to ask if you'd come in and record a demo with them."

The story spills out of me, and afterward, I feel like I've just gotten a big weight off my chest. I'd been keeping it from Aria, not maliciously or anything of the sort, for three days, trying to gauge how she'd react when I told her. Now that I have, I feel a tad better.

"Wow ... I ... don't really know what to say." Those big hazel eyes are full of astonishment. "He ... he really liked my voice?"

I nod. "And apparently, his bosses think you're brilliant as well."

"They want me to record a demo?" she breathes in a whisper, almost as if the words are reverent.

Reaching out, I set her glass down next to my own and take her hands in mine. "Yes. Here's the thing, though, love ... they want you to record three hours from now."

That was the anvil I had to drop, and when it comes crashing down upon Aria's head, she looks ready to clobber me.

"You kept this from me until three hours before I have to go sing like my bloody life is on the line?"

Across the shop, the workers, their hands full of dresses, turn their heads to investigate why Aria's voice has taken on the screechy yell of an animal that's gone mental.

"Because if I'd told you days ago, you'd have been fretting over it obsessively." She knows I am right.

Slumping back in the plush chair across from a dressing room, Aria wipes both hands down her face in pretend agony. "Jude, I can't possibly record a demo in three hours. I don't even know these people ... nor do I know if anything your record label friend is saying is true! And in three hours ... wait a minute. You're not going with me?"

At this, I have the decency to wince in shame. "Unfortunately, I'll have to be at the stadium already …"

"Kill me now. Just bloody kill me, stab the knife of embarrassment through my heart and get it over with." She sobs with exaggeration.

"We've collected a load of gorgeous dresses we think will look fab on you!" One of the shop ladies comes bouncing up.

"In you go." I wave at Aria, twirling my finger to let her know I want a full fashion show.

Although, with the sinful swaths of material the employees are holding in their hands, it will be a feat if I'm able to keep from growing hard as a steel pipe.

Before she stands to walk into the dressing room, Aria shoots me a scowl. "We're not done with this conversation."

This has me chuckling. I kind of enjoy that my girl always fights for the last word.

25

ARIA

Jude left for the stadium a half hour ago, instructing me that the driver of my car will call up to our hotel suite when it's time to leave for the recording studio.

Since the moment he told me about the phone calls he's been having with Ian Rethal, my hands haven't stopped shaking.

The tremors don't cease when the car calls up and I take the elevator down, and my legs join the quaking party in the car as we drive through the streets of London.

I can't believe Jude has left me alone to do this, scheduling it at the same time he knew he'd be getting ready for his match. Not only did the timing mean I'll be recording this demo in a room full of strangers, but it also means that I'll be late to Jude's match if this runs long. And that's the reason I'd come to London, having known nothing about this little singing session he'd covertly signed me up for. I want to see him come off the bench for RFC today, to really cheer my lungs off for him.

As Jude had suspected, our pictures from Bond Street were already trending on Twitter, and former friends of mine I haven't spoken to since my dad got sick have started texting me like we still braided each other's hair. My face has been splashed all over the Internet and is bound to be in the newspapers tomorrow morning.

Do I mind that half a billion strangers are going to begin criticizing my clothes, my hair, my looks, our relationship, and almost every other thing about me?

Honestly? Not really. I have bigger problems, and I don't live here. We may get the rare photographer in Clavering, trying to snap photos of the academy players, but no one is going to remember me enough by next week to track me down.

Plus, it's not written in stone that what Jude and I have will even last.

Pushing that sorrowful thought out of my mind, I focus on taking deep breaths in and out of my nose. I don't need Jude here; having him at the recording session will only make me feel more dependent on him than I've already become. I've forgotten over the past few weeks that I am a strong, independent woman who has taken care of a lot more in her life up until now. Recording a demo, alone, on three hours' notice, will be an easy feat.

My entire body vibrates with nerves, though, when I step out of the car and enter the building. In the middle of the sleek lobby stands the man I'm probably supposed to meet.

Ian Rethal is a slight man who looks to be in his late twenties, early thirties, with thick black-rimmed glasses and jeans tighter than mine. He's wearing an oversized leather bomber jacket and smiles with the whitest teeth I've ever seen as I walk up to him just inside the entrance of the building.

"Welcome to the studio!" He shakes my hand, and I try my best to keep my nauseous stomach in check.

"Thank you for, uh, having me." I'm not sure if that was the right thing to say.

It doesn't seem to bother Ian, who turns on his heel and

begins walking. I follow, hoping that's what he wants me to do, as he talks over his shoulder.

"When I saw you at the open mic night, I knew we had to get you in the studio. And then to find out you're dating Jude Davies? Ho ho, you'll be an overnight sensation!"

Did I want to be an overnight sensation? As we march from hallway to hallway of this posh building, I try to talk to him about my goals. "Um, well—"

Ian throws open a door, and what I always envisioned a recording studio to look like comes into view. Sleek black soundproofed walls, wood paneling, and electronic control boards with dials as far as the eye can see. Two hefty sound engineers sit at the boards and wave to Ian when he walks in. Me? They barely even glance over their shoulders to see who I am.

He cuts me off. "Here are the lyrics to the song we want you to record. I know you've never been thrown into anything like this, but it's normal."

Ian hands me pieces of papers with stanzas written on them. I look at the words, and they just look like a jumble of letters. "I'm not going to write my own song?"

Ian shakes his head. "We don't really have time for that. The executive I'm working with wants to fast track this, try to push it out to see who might be interested in managing you or signing you. He's taking a big risk on this, so we just have to work with what we have right now."

None of that means anything to me, and I feel like I am on a perpetual carnival ride that won't stop spinning. "Um, okay ..."

"Take about twenty minutes to look over those, try to memorize them, and we'll get started."

My eyes must be bugging out of my head because it feels like I am going to lose it. "Wait!"

He turns from where he is already getting down to business with the engineers. "Something wrong?"

In this situation, I feel like a little child trying to act like an adult in a room full of people way more mature than I am. When in reality, I've probably seen and had responsibilities way beyond any of these men's years. But they move faster than I do, live in a posher city, and so their actions make me feel as though I don't measure up to the level of class they exhibit.

Tilting my chin just a bit higher, I swallow my pride. "This is my first time in a studio. And while I understand the basics of what I'm supposed to do here today, you'll need to slow down. I want everything detailed out, or I won't commit to recording this demo."

Something tells me that Ian sees me as his golden ticket to a promotion, or something of the sort. He's too jittery, and by the sounds of it, is trying to fast track me to a number one single so he can write his name all over the success.

To his credit, Ian has the decency to look ashamed. "I apologize, I shouldn't have bombarded you. It's just ... your voice is special, Aria. Should have mentioned that the moment you walked in. It deserves to be heard."

Although I'm still on edge, I can tell he's being genuine. "Thank you."

"Do you want to go through the song a couple of times to work out the melody?" Ian offers.

I smile, feeling my heart rate slow down. "I'd like that, thanks."

For twenty minutes, Ian sits down with me as the engineers, who I learn are Yanis and Michael, tune up the instrumental version of the song. It was written by someone the label employs for these kinds of things, and the lyrics are so beautiful they make me want to cry. The demo Ian's having me record is a song about love and loss, with a final note of hope at the end.

"Do you think you can give it a go?" he asks patiently.

By now, my nerves have calmed to a dull roar, and the three

men in the room seem to be trying to make me as comfortable as possible. I nod, licking my suddenly dry lips, as Ian ushers me into the recording booth.

I feel like a mental patient in here, with the padded walls and my heart hammering against my ribcage. This all seems like a dream, one I never allowed myself to have. And now that it is truly happening, I can't find my wits about me.

"So, this is obviously your microphone. We're going to put headphones on you so that you can hear yourself, it makes it easier to stay in pitch. And besides that, just ... sing," Ian says as he places the headphones over my head.

I try to remember the jumble of words floating around my head, looking down at the sheet of the lyrics on the music stand in front of me. All of a sudden, the soft, slow melody of piano and guitar drifts into my headphones, and I look through the glass of the booth.

Yanis, Michael, and Ian are staring at me, and Ian holds his hand up, counting down three, two, one ...

My mouth opens, my eyes close, and without thinking, I just sing. Unworried, every emotion pouring into the story I'm telling through the lyrics, and I just let myself feel every fear, moment of passion, and sense of heartbreak.

As the music fades out, I open my eyes to the three gentlemen still staring at me.

Ian gapes at me as he says, "We may not even need another take. Get ready to be a star, love."

26

ARIA

After RFC win their game in spectacular fashion, with a goal from Jude to clinch it in the eighty-fourth minute, the boys decide it is time to celebrate.

London at night is a spectacle, all the historic buildings, twinkling lights, double-decker buses and people milling about in various states of leglessness. And on the arm of Jude, with Vance and Kingston trailing behind us, there is no door that isn't accessible.

I'm the last person to call myself a gold-digger, or someone who sought out the finer things in life, but once you have a taste of them ... it's easy to slip into the fantasy of it. Five-star meals, bottles of alcohol that cost more pounds than I could scrape up in six months and things like shop employees picking out dresses for you. It's excessive and unnecessary, yes, but these upper-crusters don't seem to care how much something cost.

Imagine that, fancying something and then buying it on the spot because you did? It's a luxury I'll never have again.

So, because I'm swept up in Jude and the world that he comes with, I let myself be carried away on the opulent tide. I put on the dress and shoes he bought me. I agree to let the hair and makeup artists into my room at the suite because I worked hard in the studio today and part of me has been waiting for this my whole life.

This is my Cinderella moment, and I'm taking it.

The four of us lounge in a big, velvet VIP booth in the back of some club I didn't catch the name of. It's on a randy row in Piccadilly Circus, and I can barely hear a thing over the music. My veins hum with the happiness of fuzzy drinks, and I am cheekily perched on Jude's lap.

A scantily clad waitress leads another group past us and parks them in the VIP section next to ours. Both Vance and Kingston's heads immediately whip to the newcomers, all of whom are gorgeous, leggy babes.

But one, in particular, seems to glow amongst the dingy darkness of the club.

This girl, or should I say goddess, has legs longer than my entire body. Her gleaming brown hair is something out of a Pantene commercial, and there is so much beauty radiating off of her, it shouldn't be legal to possess so much of it.

"Hey, you're the new Riare campaign model." Kingston points at her, leaning back on the sofa and opening his legs in a vulgar position.

Almost as if he's inviting her to sit on his lap. If I weren't so enthralled with his best friend, I'd fall for Kingston's charm. He can be boisterous and flashy, but he's got those pretty boy looks and his famous name ... I'm sure most of the girls in this bar would fall all over themselves just to sleep with him.

"And you're that cheeky football player who thinks he can bed anyone who bats an eyelash at him," the model quips back, unamused, opening a menu in her booth and chewing on a plump lip.

"Oh, I like her." My sloshed voice chuckles, and I cover my mouth with my hand.

Jude barks out a laugh while Kingston shoots me a vexing glower. The model gets up, coming over to stand near us.

"Poppy Raymond, nice to meet you." The goddess holds her hand out to me, smiling warmly, and I shake it in return.

"You look like an Amazon." I blink.

She laughs; a heavenly sound. "Good genetics pay the bills in this world, I guess. But let's face it, I'd rather look like you. You're beautiful, in a way only someone like you could be. Elegant, angelic, with the sex appeal of a loaded pistol but the grace to disguise it. When people see a woman like me, they automatically think slag or model ... my looks are far too obvious."

"Now I get it!" Kingston cries from where he sits on the other side of Jude in our booth. "You're a lesbian."

I have to really bite my tongue to keep from cracking up and the horrible job Kingston is doing trying to seduce Poppy.

The gorgeous specimen in front of us shoots Kingston a look that could melt his face off. "I'm not a lesbian. I just know how to admire beauty, in a way that doesn't scream at everyone that I'm a bloody git. However, if I were I would have ten times the game you do when trying to pick up fit birds."

"Oh my lord, I think he's met his match." Vance chuckles as he tips his beer back.

"Why don't you come sit down on my lap and find out just how much game I have." Kingston waggles his eyebrows, undeterred from her obvious distaste of him.

"Make it to the first squad, come play in London among the ranks of the big boys, and maybe I'll give your theory a test." Poppy smirks and flounces back to her booth.

She's only just on the other side of the raised velvet booth, but by the way she just shut Kingston down, you'd think he'd have just watched a girl catapult herself to the other side of the world using a circus cannon.

That is how stunned Kingston Phillips is.

"Shake it off, brother." Vance claps a big hand down on his friend's shoulder.

Sensing an explosion coming on, Jude interrupts before Kingston can blow up. "Hey, let's go somewhere else, yeah? This place is starting to get lame."

He must agree, I can't hear the rest of their conversation over the boom of the music, but we are suddenly leaving in a flurry of motion and people. We leave the club with triple the number of people we came in with, and the group trails behind the three golden boys, with me attached to Jude's side.

As we all stand on the pavement, Kingston still won't stop complaining to Vance about what Poppy said to him.

"Did you hear her, mate? Turning down the likes of me? Does she even know who I am?" His pouty lips hang open incredulously.

And just as I think he's about to go back in and get her, Jude whistles to his friend, who saunters over to him.

The scene that plays out next is something out of a teen cult classic.

Jude flags down a bus while Kingston practically stands in the middle of the road to get it to stop. These boys are a bunch of mad nutters, but I'm sloshed and mesmerized by their world, so I just wobble here and chuckle watching them.

Is this what it feels like to be young, wild, and free? Like that Wiz Khalifa song claims it is?

My four-inch heels, the ones Jude surprised me with, dig into the London pavement as I throw my arms up and do a twirl. The sparkly gold dress that I picked off the rack, at the store I would never have dreamed of walking into but did with Jude's insistence, creeps up my thighs. It already barely graces them anyway, and with my giddy dance move, I've probably flashed the entire country. But right now, I don't care in the slightest.

I'm out, in a major city, with the boy I have a major crush on, full of fruity liquor and dancing in a mini-dress that costs more than one month of our mortgage. If this isn't a time to celebrate, I don't know when I'll ever get one again.

"Are you twirling?" Jude smirks as he catches me around the waist.

The world takes a moment to right itself before I can answer him. "And what if I am?"

"I'd say that it's adorable."

Sucking my lower lip in, I pout. "I don't want to be adorable. I want to be sexy."

Now he leans in, nipping the lobe of my ear with his teeth, and whispers, "Oh, love, you don't need to worry about that. I've never seen a sexier creature in my life."

Well, that's one way to get a girl between the sheets. Lord, my body erupts in goose bumps as I press myself to him. Suddenly, the fur coat he also bought me is way too warm, and I wish there weren't a crowd of people around us. Because I feel the distinct need to be alone with Jude at this moment.

"I got one!" Kingston yells from the street, cars narrowly missing his burly form.

Slowing down, as not to crush Jude's friend under its two-decker weight, a bus comes to a stop in front of England's future left back.

"Why aren't his lights on?" I ask daftly.

Jude lets his hands graze over my bum. "He's off the clock. Watch this."

He winks back at me as he and Kingston saunter toward the bus.

"You know who we are, mate?" Kingston says to the driver of the bus as the doors screech open.

The bloke, a frumpish man who looks like he's had a long day of work, seems as though he might have swallowed his tongue. His eyes bulge out as he takes in Jude, Kingston, and Vance, plus the assortment of a dozen other flashy partiers.

"Um ... well, of course ..."

Vance pulls out a wad of money, pound notes further than the eye can see. "We'll give you all of this up front, plus a bonus after, if you keep your lights off, drive us around the city, allow us to play music and imbibe, all while keeping this quiet and out of the papers."

Wait a second ...

"We're going to commandeer a double-decker bus for our own party?" I blink up at Jude.

"Welcome to the posh kid's club." Those dazzling green eyes wink at me once more.

Everyone piles onto the bus after Vance completes the deal with the driver, and off we go.

The lights shut off as he winds the big double-decker around the corner of a building, and then the behemoth vehicle picks up speed, zooming by the electric energy of downtown London. I can't help but climb to the second level and feel Jude's hands come around my waist as he assists me up.

The newest Beyoncé song starts to vibrate through the bus, and someone must have convinced the driver to let them hijack the sound system. As we reach the second level, several people come up behind us, handles of alcohol rattling in their fingers as they climb. Drinks start to flow, with our companions taking swigs right out of the bottle.

I press myself into a seat at the front of the bus, staring out the window as my sloshed mind tries to keep up. I'm sitting on the edge of the world, or so it seems, with no barrier between my body and the glass.

"Wild, isn't it?" Jude slides in next to me.

The colors catch his face as we drive through the city on our pirate vehicle. He's intense and beautiful, staring at me as if I could be his last meal.

"Nothing is ever tame when I'm with you," I tell him truthfully, the alcohol loosening my tongue.

And as if it isn't loose enough, Jude bends his head to mine and makes our mouths tangle in an impassioned kiss. The kind of kiss that can only be had when drinks are involved and you're doing something reckless.

The way our lips stoke the fire burning deep in my belly only further flames the hellion in me.

Making out with Jude as we race through the city in stolen transportation, a party going on all around us, is easily the most insane thing I've ever done.

And if insanity has overtaken me, I am going to let it. Jude Davies makes it too addicting to be stable.

27

ARIA

"You lot aren't coming to Praise?"

Kingston asks as Jude and I enter the kitchen, still in our pajamas. Vance is sitting at the table, eating porridge and eggs, next to some brunette he brought on the bus last night, and she's wearing an enormous T-shirt which I can only guess is his. She's scrolling through her phone over the coffee cup pressed to her lips, as sunshine streams through the hotel suite.

I blush thinking about the definite possibility of them having sex last night and wonder how she'll get home this morning. I'm not completely daft, I know what a one-night stand is and how girls do walks of shame. But ... I've been living under a rock trying to save my father's life for almost two years and gossiping with friends about shagging has not been on the agenda. I'm just not used to this casual kind of interaction.

"No, we're not coming. You'll have to worship without me ... some of us played a huge match and recorded a song yesterday, and we're knackered," Jude answers for us.

"Kingston ... you go to church?" I'm thoroughly confused at this.

I'm sure it's something his parents expect of him when he's home, but for Kingston to put on his Sunday's best and venture into a religious building this early in the day is ... well, shocking.

The brunette at the table snickers. "Praise isn't a church. It's a club. Only open on Sunday mornings, from seven a.m. to noon, and it's epic. We tagging along?"

Her question is directed at Vance, who regards her with what I'd say is almost zero interest, but he nods anyway.

"A club? That is only open on Sunday? Blimey, how do they make any money?" The concept of this is so foreign to me, I almost can't believe it.

"Because there are about a thousand people there a week, and they're running all kinds of illegal drugs through it. Every person in the club is either high or rolling," Kingston answers, pouring himself some orange juice.

I watch in awe as he adds champagne to it, and I can't fathom how these people can still be drinking, let alone thinking about going out to a club within the hour.

"Rolling?" I look up at Jude.

"High on ecstasy," he answers.

And suddenly, I'm glad he asked me back in our room if I just wanted to stay at the hotel suite for a few hours by ourselves. Yes, our room. Jude wouldn't hear of it last night when I suggested sleeping in the fourth room in the suite. He dragged me to his bed, wrapped me in his arms, and we fell into the kind of peaceful snooze that only a lot of alcohol can bring.

We have to go back to Clavering around three p.m., and I have been looking forward to some downtime, or maybe a nice bath in the big porcelain tub in the en suite bathroom. To hear that Praise is a place where a lot of drugs are being taken doesn't make me feel comfortable, and I am appreciative that Jude wants to avoid it.

I lean into him as he juts a hip onto the marble island of the hotel kitchen, loving the warmth of his shirtless skin. The soft pajama bottoms that hang low on his hips are tantalizing, and suddenly, I'm not very hungry for breakfast.

Holding me to him, we walk in tandem to the electric kettle where he pours hot water into two mugs and places tea bags in them to steep.

"Milk?" he asks, leaving me at the counter and walking to the fridge.

I blush, seeing him walk around shirtless. "Yes, please. And a bit of honey."

Asking someone how they take their tea is such an intimate act. The fact that Jude is making mine means he wants to memorize it. That notion makes my stomach and heart flip at the exact same time.

Behind us, Kingston snorts. "All right, you ready? Let's get out of here before I choke on my tongue from all the dishy ridiculousness."

Vance clears his breakfast plates and follows Kingston out the door, with the girl right on their heels. The two of them don't even ask as if they care if she accompanies them, and I roll my eyes at their disinterest.

And then it's just Jude and me, alone in this big hotel suite.

"Hungry?" he asks me.

Why can he only seem to speak in one-word sentences this morning?

I shrug, the air between us growing heavier with electricity by the second. We shared a bed all last night, and yet both of us had an unspoken agreement that nothing should happen. We were pissed, tired, and mentally exhausted from the debauchery of the night. While it was impossible not to feel along the silky crevices of Jude's ab muscles as he held me close, there had been some trepidation. I know I'm was ready to sleep with him, but not when something was altering my mind.

"I could eat." I throw it out to gauge is mood.

Something about Jude makes me want to abandon all of my principles. I'm not the type of girl who would have sex with a boy she's only known a few months, much less in broad daylight in a fancy hotel suite. I'm also not the type of girl who'd leave her sick father at home to go gallivanting in London and get sloshed on a double-decker that said boy basically hijacked. Yet, here I am.

My heart begins to beat double time as Jude strides toward me, closing the small gap between us. Every ounce of saliva in my mouth disappears as his bare chest and arms press my body into them, and my knees are trembling I am so nervous.

Looking up into his blazing green eyes, I speak the thought that's overwhelming me. "Jude ... I know that you know I'm not a virgin. But, I'm also not ... as experienced as you."

One big hand comes up to palm my cheek, his thumb brushing back and forth on the bone there. "Good. Because when I take you into that bedroom, I want to leave my mark on your body, and your mind. One you'll never be able to scrub off. You'll never be able to forget the first time we came together."

Now, instead of worrying about his past trysts, all I can see is red. Warm, hot, pulsing, the color of passion and hearts and sin. Jude paints my world in it, and all of my anxiety is replaced by scarlet arousal.

Taking my hand in his, Jude leads me back to the bedroom we shared the night before. The shades and curtains are still drawn, with muted light falling onto the carpeted floor and bed. It's the perfect Sunday morning hue, and the tightening between my legs trumps any self-conscious thoughts about getting naked in front of him without all the lights off.

Jude sits down on the edge of the bed, his legs spread lazily, his naked chest dancing in front of my eyes, begging to be explored. Still grasping my fingers in his, he drags me gently to nestle in his thighs and put my hand on that perfect torso.

There are no questions in his eyes or on his tongue, and I remember that he said he wouldn't ask me if I was sure. I know that once we start this, he won't stop. He knows, just by gazing at me, that I am ready and don't need to be checked upon like a child.

My fingertips trail over every inch of muscle and raw maleness, tangling gently in the smattering of jet black hair that disappears below the waistband of his pajama pants. The place where ego lives in my chest swells with pride when a groan springs free of his lips as one of my thumbs hooks in the elastic of the flannel.

"Not just yet," Jude murmurs to himself before pulling me in and crushing our lips together.

Falling backward onto the mattress, he pulls me with him so I have no choice but to straddle his waist as his tongue invades my mouth. In long, slow kisses, Jude coaxes the fire he started within me to rage and burn at an impossible level. After only a minute or two, I am writhing on top of him, grinding myself into the erection pressing into the most sensitive part of me.

Skillfully, Jude pulls my top over my head, my moan echoing between us like a relieved thank you. The simple sports bra I'd donned beneath comes off next, and my nipples harden to tight peaks with anticipatory longing.

"So gorgeous ..." Jude trails off, turning all of his attention to the objects of affection dangling in front of his face.

It's all I can do to keep myself upright and my elbows locked as he takes each rigid bud in his mouth. As his tongue traces the trail of his saliva over my breasts, I am rendered helpless, mewling on top of him as my head tips back and I rub back and forth on his steel arousal.

"Pants ... off ..." I can't even form a sentence as I beg him for relief.

It has been so long since I've been touched like this, and never in my life has it been this deftly. Jude knows secrets about my body that even I don't, and my one and only experience with sex had been a fumbling attempt with puppy love folded into it. I almost forgot how to be physical with a boy, because it has been years.

Jude is catching me right back up to speed and surpassing all the fantasies I had about him leading up to this. Flipping me over, he tosses me up the bed, at the top near the pillows, like I weigh two kilograms. Following me as I scoot back, the man looks like some kind of natural-born predator about to take a bite out of his prey.

His eyes are blazing a dark shade of emerald that don't seem fair to possess. All of that dark hair on his head is mussed and crazed, and all I want to do is tangle my hands back in it. Those big hands grip my ankle, and then my thigh, reaching for the hem of my sleep shorts and pulling them off in one fell swoop.

The only thing that stands between me and complete nakedness is the simple cotton underwear I'm still wearing.

Jude curses under his breath as he takes me in. "You may not be a virgin, but bloody hell are you virginal. I can't wait to defile that."

They're filthy, his words, and I shock myself realizing that everything below my waist flushes at them. Who knew I'd be so turned on by dirty language, but for some reason, the sentiments Jude is growling out make me wetter than I've ever been before.

In a split second, my underwear is off, joining the rest of my clothes on the floor. Jude sucks in a ragged breath as my own lungs struggle to keep functioning. The molten lust in his eyes would knock me off my feet if I weren't already lying down, and when he begins to lower himself to the apex of my thighs, my consciousness threatens to give out.

With a testing swipe of his tongue across my most private parts, Jude smiles a devilish grin up at my wide eyes. "The sweetest thing I've ever tasted."

And then, he feasts on me.

His mouth and tongue do things to my anatomy that I've never even heard of before. I can do little more than grip the sheets and cry out with pleasure. No one has ever done this to me before, and I squeeze my eyes shut as sensations assault me.

Tighter and tighter, the coil within me twists until I'm almost blind with the need for release. Sensing it, Jude stops, and I whine my protest.

"Easy, love. I want you to come around my cock," he soothes, removing his pants and briefs in one effortless move.

I'm stunned as I look at the size of him. I've popped my cherry, but I'm not sure he'll fit with how large he is and how long it's been. Without having a conversation about it, Jude grabs a condom from a bag on the floor and rolls it on, hissing as he pinches the tip.

My legs spread instinctively as he joins me again in the center of the bed, and I'm so wet between my thighs that I can't stop rolling my hips in search of relief.

"Has a man ever made you come before?" he asks in a deadly quiet whisper as he lines himself up to my entrance.

I shake my head, too wound up with nerves and a split second away from an orgasm to speak.

"Good. I want to be the one to give that to you."

Jude drives into me in a fluid stroke, seating himself deeply. The pain and pleasure mix and I throw my head back into the pillows. There are no more words between us, just moans and the sounds of slapping flesh. Sex noises, the kind that are animalistic and primal.

My hands grip his back as he invades me, pushing in over and over again with torturous speed. Slow enough that I feel every ridge of his huge organ against my folds, but fast enough that I can't catch my breath.

When I lost my virginity, and the couple of times my secondary school boyfriend and I had sex after that, I hadn't experienced an orgasm. I've only ever given them to myself a handful of times, the result of living in a small row home held together by paper-thin walls, with my father not to mention.

I've never experienced a climax at the hands of a partner. It's the second to last thought that occupies my brain before Jude strokes in deep, the blunt pad of his thumb pressing sharply against my clit.

And then I am floating, high up in the clouds where my limbs feel every nerve ending imaginable and my brain goes numb. This feeling, this pure bliss that only vibrates out to every cell as Jude pounds into me, is unlike any other I've felt before.

I register Jude stilling as a tremendous growl rips from his throat, and he buries his face in my neck. Inside me, his member twitches and I know he's joining me in my stages of euphoria.

As the effects wind down, and my mind settles into the post-coital haze, the last thought before my orgasm hits me once more.

Jude is the only man I ever want to make me feel this way.

28

JUDE

My mind is blown.

Utterly and completely destroyed.

Even hours after I'd been forced to leave the bed where Aria lay naked, I can't seem to assemble my jumbled thoughts.

The smell of her lingered on me even as I drove to the location Barry insisted I meet him. My mind got lost thinking about how I'd explored every inch of Aria's body, and the ways she enchanted my heart.

It's true, I've been with plenty of women before her. She even said as much when that shy, innocent face was trying to convey explicitly how inexperienced she is.

Blimey, does she have any idea how she just erased every girl who came before her?

And the way she orgasmed, her inner muscles tightening around me as those angelic eyes fluttered shut on a blissful sigh. I feel my knob hardening just thinking about how her gorgeous face looked at that moment.

I should have known how much trouble I was in before I

took her to bed, but I hadn't been thinking of much else except seeing Aria naked for the first time.

The damage is done now, though. I am more than smitten ... I have fallen into her. It's been happening for a while, the slow slide of my heart conjoining with hers. No one else possesses me like Aria does, and with this final act of shedding any barriers between us ... the collide has happened.

How am I to tell her? Does she know? Better yet, does she feel the same?

As a cocky shite, I've always clung to my freedom. Relationships and commitment are the enemies. It's almost laughable; the universe playing a funny trick on me, that my reserve had collapsed so quickly when Aria walked into my world.

Begrudgingly, I get out of the black car Barry sent when it arrives at the location he specified. I am a little more than annoyed that he interrupted my day in bed with Aria to demand I meet him for lunch. It meant having to forgo a second round with my girlfriend and taking the ride back to Clavering with her.

She had to work, and so was forced to take the town car home by herself while I stayed back in London.

"You're a real git, you know that?" I curse my publicist as I walk into the restaurant.

It's a real old-school type place, something out of *Goodfellas* or *Boondock Saints*.

"I wanted you to have lunch with someone." Barry stands, obscuring the other diner from view.

Shaking his hand, I speak in a clipped tone. "You know I have to get back to the academy or Harrington will have my balls."

"I don't think old Niles will mind if he knew you were having lunch with me."

Peering around Barry to discover who spoke, I almost drop

to the floor with surprise. Standing in front of a pushed out chair with a glass of stock in his hand, is none other than Killian Ramsey.

I'm not the kind of man to be shocked easily, or in awe of someone. I play on a world's stage with its superstars and puppeteers almost every week, and my life has been that way since I can remember.

But having Killian Ramsey standing two feet in front of me … I'm as big of a fanboy as can be found.

This man is a legend. He is *the* football player. Killian Ramsey holds all the titles, he's the player I've always looked up to, the one I watched on TV at the academy and who all of my friends want to play as when we put FIFA in the video game console.

Killian brought honor to England and set me down a path where I wanted to accomplish the same.

"Mr. Ramsey … it's nice to meet you, sir." Who the hell is this blubbering idiot I've been replaced with?

And since when do I call people *sir*?

Killian chuckles. "I'm not your father, boy. Call me Killian. Seems you'll be trying to erase my records in those holy football books, so you might as well call me by my first name."

"Killian, then. I'm Jude, by the way."

"He knows who you are, or he wouldn't have asked to meet with you." Barry snorts and rolls his eyes. "I'll leave you two to it."

With that, my publicist walks out of the room, and Killian gestures for me to have a seat across the table from him. A waiter appears out of nowhere, setting down a glass in front of each of us. From the smell coming off them, it's definitely scotch.

"You wanted to meet with me?" I ask him as plates are placed in front of us.

Typically, a T-bone steak such as this, with a side of steaming potatoes and green beans, would be half-finished in three seconds flat. But I'm too nervous to eat, a feat not typical for me. I guess sitting in front of my hero will do that.

Killian nods slowly, cutting into his steak. "I've been watching you for a while now, Jude. You're a hell of a football player. Probably better than me, though if you tell anyone I said that, I'll deny it."

I almost choke on my tongue. "Th-thank you. But you're wrong. The matches you've played ... you're the man to beat."

"I have a feeling you might beat me. But that's not why I brought you here ... your ego is stroked enough by the entire bloody country."

That has me chuckling because he isn't wrong. Though what he says next slaps the smile right off my face.

"I feel as if it's my duty, as England's former great player to its next prodigy, to ask you why the bloody hell you're allowing your life off the pitch to affect the one on it?"

My stomach drops as the tips of my ears begin to burn. Shame and anger mix into one potent combination, setting my heart pounding as I try to calm myself enough to answer him.

"I don't see what my personal life has to do with how I play," I grit out.

Killian chuckles. "And that's why we're here. You've been horsing around with your friends for too long. You should have been playing for RFC two years ago, but you can't keep your act together long enough for Niles to trust you won't kill yourself on the big boy stage in London."

Folding my arms over my chest, my answer is almost pouty. "I've been doing better, starting games for them."

"Only because the Rogue owners threatened to sell you," he retorts.

How did he know that?

"The girl you're pictured everywhere with ... is she your

cover? The thing that will make you appear to be a reformed bad boy?" Killian sips his drink, eyeing me knowingly across the table.

I can feel my jaw tense with annoyance. He can pick at me all day long, but now he wants to poke holes in my relationship? He wants to go after Aria? I don't care who he is, I'll rip his throat out.

"Don't speak about her like that."

He nods, a small smile on his lips. He doesn't speak for a minute or so. "So you love her, then?"

Something inside my chest loosens because thus far, I haven't put a name to what Aria makes me feel. Hearing Killian say it ... I know that I am. But he doesn't need to be privy to that information.

"Why are we talking about this?" I frown.

Aria is none of his business, just like she's no one else's business. If I want to have a girlfriend, I can have one without detailing every aspect of our relationship out to every bloody citizen under the Queen's rule.

"Because she's in this now ... Aria, that's her name, right? You made her a part of this circus you're about to embark on, simply by holding her hand yesterday on Bond Street. You're a smart chap, Jude, you wouldn't have done it if you weren't, one, using her as a good girl cover to make yourself look better to Niles. Or two, if you were really in love with her. I'm going with number two, because from your attitude alone, I can distinctly tell you don't give a rat's arse what Niles or the country thinks of you."

I gulp down my glass of water and wipe my lips. "Well, you've got one thing right about me."

Killian tilts his head, regarding me while my jaw clicks as I try to keep my temper at bay.

"I used to be exactly like you, Jude. A hothead, angry at the world for taking the people I love most away from me. I knew everything, and fuck anyone who tried to tell me I didn't. I was in a dark place for a very long time, and both my playing and my life suffered because of it. It took me too long to dig myself out of it, and when I met my wife, it was clear I needed to straighten up. You think you can walk around London like you bloody own the place, getting into trouble and acting like a cocky arse with your friends. *You're wasting time*! Jude, you can be one of the greatest talents this sport has ever seen. But if you keep pissing away your God-given ability out in Clavering because you can't keep your nose clean long enough to let Niles promote you to the first squad, then you're a bigger twit than I thought you were!"

His open palm slams down on the table, and I'm left stunned. I've forgotten ...

For almost ten years, I've lived as the only adult in my world. I took care of my little brothers, but I had no one to answer to. No one has spoken to me, like Killian just did, in a very long time. My parents are gone, and with them, they took any life lessons to be learned or any guidance to be taken.

"I've been trying ..." I say weakly to the tabletop, finally succumbing to the humbling he's trying to give me.

When I look up at him, his eyes are a little less clouded with rage. "Lost my temper there for a minute, see? I forget at times that I'm now a family man and a role model. Something you should aspire to be because you have all the capacity to get there. If you're trying to be better, keep trying. And keep your Aria around ... from how protective you got, like a rabid dog with a bone, I can tell you love her. She'll be a guiding force of light in your life, don't squander that."

Killian's advice, as daft as it sounds, allows something to click in me. He's right, it's time to abandon the ways of a naughty boy and become a man. Both on the pitch, off of it, and where Aria is concerned.

29

ARIA

"Would you like to have tea with me?" Jude asks me as his hand runs up and down my arm.

Jude's question comes as he's walking me home after his last practice of the day. It's a Sunday, a day I shouldn't be at the academy, but Patricia had some extra work and I could always use the pay, so I agreed to go into the sew house.

It's been two weeks since we arrived back to Clavering from London. And I'm not sure what happened at that lunch Jude told me he had with Killian Ramsey ... but the football legend must have smacked some sense into my boyfriend because he's been as angelic as the winged creatures in heaven.

Jude has been attentive, kind, studious in class and a force to be reckoned with on the pitch. He's asked about my father, treated us to dinner, stayed in his dorm room both Friday nights with me after I got off shift, and just seems like a completely different person. Well, not completely different ... he's still got the biggest ego I've ever seen, besides Kingston, and can make me blush with just one dirty sentence.

"Um … sure. Right now? Because I kind of wanted a nap," I confess.

"Well, actually, yes, right now. You could nap on the drive? It's about half an hour."

I tilt my head as we walk along, our interlocked hands swinging between us. "Oh? And where is this tea we're attending?"

Jude smiles. "It's with my brothers, at our family home."

My breath halts in my lungs. "You want me to meet your brothers?"

"Yes. Should we walk back to my car?" Jude turns us back up the road and I follow along as my thoughts race at a hundred kilometers an hour.

That's a big step, meeting his brothers. Jude rarely talks about his family, or his parent's death, and I can only imagine what has possessed him to ask me to tea today with his relatives.

I can somewhat imagine the responsibility on his shoulders to care for his little brothers, a similarity between us that actually makes us rather well-suited for one another. But … it's different. Jude has cared for two people who could barely care for themselves for much longer than I've been caring for my dad. With Dad, he can tell me all the ways he needs help. He has the knowledge of health care, of paying bills, of … life in general. Jude had to take on looking after not only his childhood self, but two other children. His brothers were just babies when their parent's died.

And now he wants to bring me into his world, the one he let no one else see. To say that I am nervous would be an understatement.

We climb into Jude's BMW that is parked on the side of the academy grounds closest to the road leading to my home.

"I get to pick the music," I tease as we buckle our seatbelts.

He nods, picking up my hand to kiss it. "I wouldn't argue with that, you always have better taste in song choice anyway."

I haven't heard much from Ian about the demo. I've checked in three times, and he says he's still cutting it to make it perfect, and/or trying to pitch it to higher-ups. Trying not to let the hope reach my heart has been the most difficult thing I've done in a while, because if it's received even decently well ... it could change my family's life.

As Jude winds the car out of the academy gates and through the streets of Clavering, I pick up his phone to scroll through his music selections. He's only let me do this a handful of times, mostly because I think he's embarrassed that his music library only has about three hundred songs and my old iPod contains over three thousand.

"Marilyn Manson ... really?" I raise an eyebrow at him, bemused.

Jude shrugs those big, brawny shoulders. "I liked one of his songs once and added the rest for good measure."

It's not my taste, so I keep scrolling. Until I land on one of my favorite songs. The opening chords of "Rhiannon" by Fleetwood Mac start to play over the state-of-the-art sound system, and Jude looks to me with a megawatt smile on his face.

"She is like a cat in the dark and then she is the darkness. She rules her life like a fine skylark and when the sky is starless," he sings, drumming his hands on the steering wheel.

I'm a little shocked that he knows one of my favorite songs, and I sing along. A minute into the song, Jude pulls one of his hands from the wheel to stroke it through my hair, and I lean into his palm.

The rest of the short trip is spent singing along quietly to songs I pick, and by the time we pull up in front of a quaint home three towns over, I've forgotten all about how nervous I was.

The moment Jude steps a foot outside of the car, the front door of the house opens and two gangly boys come running out.

"Jude!" the smaller one yells, clearly not old enough to be embarrassed about catching his brother up in a hug.

I get out, standing there as a grin splits my mouth watching Jude greet his siblings. They're all clones of each other, and I can immediately see what teenage, and young child Jude looked like. These two are going to be heartbreakers just like their brother.

"Mates, I want you to meet my girlfriend, Aria." He waves me over.

"She's really pretty," Jude's younger brother Charlie says candidly.

I can't help the chuckle that leaves my throat. "Well, thank you. It's lovely to meet you."

We shake hands, and I turn to Paul, the fourteen-year-old. You could tell he is in that stage, the sullen teenage one where he isn't quite sure what to do with the new feelings coursing through him or the way his body is growing like a weed. He's in that awkward stage, the one all teens go through and then forget about because it's nasty business. I hated my own if I'm being honest.

"Paul, I'm very glad I get to meet you." I nod at him.

He tentatively nods, which I'll take as a warm greeting, before turning to Jude and enveloping him in a hug. I haven't known the boy more than two seconds and I can tell that he needs the most love and comfort. That he counts on Jude even more than Jude counts on himself.

"Shall we come in?" A woman appears at the door, and I know this must be the aunt who takes care of the younger boys.

After introductions are made, we all sit down to tea in the living room. Paul and Charlie tell Jude about what's going on at school, their new favorite movies, the outcomes of their individual football games and ask him about his last match in London. Jude's aunt Tilda and uncle Brenner ask me about my job, home, and family. I give vague, amicable answers ... because no one needs my sob story bringing the mood of the day down.

Once the teacups are empty and we're all a bit talked out, Jude takes me for a tour around the house. It's not quite a cottage, and yet it isn't a mansion. It's a middle-sized family home, but you can tell some of the bells and whistles have been added. Posh countertops, a sunken tub in the master bedroom, a swimming pool out back ... it's clear Jude has spared no expense for his family.

"Is this ... is this your childhood home?" I wonder, looking at the pictures on the wall going down the stairs.

If it were his aunt and uncle's place, they'd have pictures of themselves. But these photos, the ones hanging in frames everywhere, are of a different couple ... two people who are the perfect combination of Jude.

"Yes, sort of. The grief counselor the court mandated after my parent's died thought it would be best for Paul and Charlie to keep living in their own home. My aunt and uncle were close by and didn't object, so they sold their home and moved into ours. But ... this isn't *my* childhood home. It's the one my parents purchased after my first decent contract came through."

I cock my head to the side. "Does it ever bother you? That your parents lived well because of your money? That your brothers do now?"

He shrugs and says his next words as if they make the most sense in the world. "No. They are my family."

Skimming my fingers over the three Davies brothers as little boys, I speak but don't look at him. "Sometimes it bothers me ... in my family situation."

"That's because your mother only left, and my parents died."

His harsh sentiment slaps me square in the face. "Wha ...?"

Jude laces his fingers in mine. "You know I'm not great with the whole sensitivity thing … but I don't mean that as an offense."

"Sure felt like one," I mumble, a lump of shame forming in my throat.

"I mean, that our situations are different. I have no problem supporting my brothers because our parents died. Left this earth without their own consent. You resent the situation you're in because with another mother, one who deserved a daughter like you, you wouldn't have to be doing it alone. There would be a parent there with you, helping to pay for your family's bills. I don't blame you for being angry, in fact, if I were you, I'd be furious. I'm not trying to be harsh, I'm trying to tell you that I admire the shite out of you for being in an impossible situation and making it work."

His answer both stuns me and makes my heart melt. While being completely transparent and honest, Jude has managed not only to give me an insight into his own situation but commend me on the job I'm doing for my family.

Closing the space between us, I push up on my toes and gently press a kiss to his cheek. I let my mouth linger there, to drink in his scent, and I feel his eyelashes flutter closed on my opposite cheek.

"Thank you."

He pulls back, and my heart jumps into my throat. Because the look he's giving me, one of intense emotion that so closely mirrors the words I've been keeping inside … it's almost as if he's going to tell me he loves me.

I wait with bated breath for him to utter the sentiment I've been trying not to blurt out.

"Jude! Come play a bit of footie out back!"

Charlie's voice interrupts the moment, and Jude drops the hand that was about to smooth back a lock of my hair.

"We should go see what he's up to," Jude says quietly, seeming to be having an internal war with himself.

I nod and follow him out, trying not to let my pounding, disappointed heart get the best of me. I'm not brave enough to say it first, either.

But I can see that Jude is changing, and he is transforming into what might just be the perfect man the universe could have ever sent to me.

30

ARIA

Two more weeks pass, with Jude going to London for both of RFC's matches.

He starts, scores three goals between the two games, and the papers herald him as finally coming into his own. I know now that it's just a matter of time before Niles Harrington calls him up for good, but I try to push it to the back of my mind.

My life stays the same, mostly; I go to work; I come home to take care of my father, and then I go back to work. Jude has offered thrice more to take some of the monetary burden off my back by paying for Dad's hospital bills, but I refuse. Even though I love him—not that I've told him yet—I won't be beholden to him.

Jude left for London yesterday to play a mid-week game, and I find myself at home on a very rare night off. There is a soiree at the academy tonight, which means a catering staff will be responsible for cleanup for the night. I am taking the opportunity to just ... relax, a novel concept for me. Which I am probably failing at because, currently, I've thrown the contents of my dresser onto my bed to sort and fold.

In the next instant, my bedroom door opens and I nearly fall on the floor.

"Wha ... what are you ... how are you in my bedroom?"

Jude makes my room look miniature, that's how much space he takes up. All of that gorgeous caramel skin and jet-black hair intimidates my measly twin bed and old rickety desk as he stands in the doorway.

"Well, I walked down the road from the academy, rang your bell, asked your father if you were home, and poof, here I am!"

I scowl at him. "I'm aware of how humans transport themselves. I'm asking how you found out my address. And aren't you supposed to be in London?"

In all the time we've been together, I've always hidden my home from Jude. I never told him where our row house is, and that was done purposely, as I never wanted him to witness the kind of poverty I come from.

"Country? I didn't know English people liked this genre of music." Jude ignores my questions and observes my ancient, second-hand laptop, which is pumping Old Dominion's "One Man Band" through its pathetic speakers.

I shrug. "Music is music, in my opinion. I love the lead singer's voice, and the song is catchy."

Part of me wants to run around the room, cleaning up or shoving things in drawers, but I know it will do no good. My room will still be a dingy, musty, tiny space that is embarrassingly less decadent than any place Jude has ever stayed.

"Aria, stop fretting," he says without looking at me as he walks around my room. Though ... how he can walk three steps without hitting a wall, I'm not sure.

When I begin to chew my lip, Jude crosses to me and swipes his thumb across it so that I release the skin from my teeth.

"Whatever you're thinking I think about the place you call home, I'm not. I think this is just a place, and it has nothing to do with how wonderful you are. So, stop worrying that I'm judging you, or that you need to impress me. I think we're far past that. Yes?"

Now his hands are buried in my hair as he tilts my head to look up at him. I nod, fisting my hands in his shirt and pulling him down as he pulls me up. Our mouths meet, and suddenly, the tense worry I felt just seconds before evaporates into an intense need to get as close to Jude as possible.

"When you leave, I miss you terribly," I whisper, my most secret thought slipping out.

"Being away from you is torture," he agrees, slanting his head more so that he can plunge his tongue deeper into my mouth.

Without preamble, Jude lifts me like a feather onto the small desk in my room, spreading my knees with his big hands and stepping into the embrace of my legs. I wrap them around his waist as we dissolve into moaning, lust-filled creatures.

Backing off, with breathing so ragged I'm afraid he might pass out, Jude's eyes blaze into mine. Will this be the moment he tells me he loves me?

"With a single look, you can bring me to my knees." Jude sinks to the floor instead.

My mouth goes dry and falls right open. "Me?"

"Yes, you. Only ever you."

It's a heady thing, having Jude Davies tell you you're the only woman he'd ever get on his knees for.

It might not be a club in London or an airplane ride to New York or the freaking Grammys, for all I know he's been to those somehow ... but initiating in foreplay with the most gorgeous specimen I've ever encountered while my father watches TV downstairs is ...exciting. That sounds wonky, but it's a risky business that I get turned on from. The fact that Jude and I have to be quiet as he unbuttons my jeans and pulls them down my legs, that I have to slap a hand over my mouth as he licks up the seam of my core, that my hips are clamped down so hard by his nimble fingers as to keep them from wiggling the rickety old desk.

That he can't make a noise when I push my hand past the elastic of his boxers to brush the tip of his hard cock.

Why is having sex so much more illicit when there is the possibility of being caught in the act? Why does holding your moans in your throat make the impending orgasm that much more exciting to reach?

Jude grinds his tool into me at a slow, mind-numbing pace. He's holding himself back, so much that I can feel his shoulders trembling beneath my arms where I grip them around his neck.

"Come for me," he whispers in my ear, teasing a hand between us and rolling my clit between his thumb and forefinger.

At the angle he's penetrating me at, it's all I can do to keep quiet. It's so good, *so good,* but I just need a little bit more.

"Harder ... please ..." I gasp.

A trickle of sweat beads on Jude's brow as he pulls back ever so slightly, smirking. "You have no idea what you just asked for."

I have to stifle a yelp as Jude lifts me from the desk, holding me in midair, while he's still buried deep inside of me.

"Now we won't make noise on the desk, but you have to promise to be a good girl and keep quiet," he taunts me.

As he starts to move, picking up the pace, I have to bite down on the sensitive skin of his neck to keep from screaming in pleasure. Jude holds me under both knees, plunging my body onto his cock as if I were nothing more than a doll for his eventual release. In this instant, I couldn't care less how objectifying that might be ... all I can think about is the orgasm that is about to smack me over the head.

And then Jude slams me down once more, hitting the exact

spot that sends me combusting into a million tiny pieces. I have to bury my face in his neck and swallow the wail that rises from my throat, the sensations of my climax rolling on and on as Jude keeps his punishing pace before stilling to surrender to his own release. I can feel the rumble of his chest as he grips me tighter to him, the growl he wants to roar into the air held back only by the lips planted to my scalp.

In the middle of my tiny bedroom, he holds me up while the world itself floats away, leaving only the two of us.

31

ARIA

Jude is still hovering over me, where he set me back down on the desk to catch his breath, when he says, "Niles Harrington asked me to go to London, permanently. I'm going to be the starting forward for RFC."

At that exact moment, my heart shatters into a thousand pieces before dropping to my feet. Even though he is still inside me, it already feels as if Jude is a million miles away.

"You came here to have sex with me one last time?" I gape at him, too shocked to push him off me.

"That's not what this is at all and you know it." He glowers, but steps away from me, tucking himself back into his pants and straightening his clothes.

Suddenly, I feel overly conscious of my disheveled, half-nude state. I gingerly jump down from the desk and begin to straighten myself and pull my clothes on. Something about the air in the room, the sharp change from borderline love to betrayal, makes the whole encounter feel like a cheap one-night stand instead of a sexy tryst with your boyfriend.

I am trying not to look at Jude, because if I do, I know I'll start to cry. "But you did want to fuck me one more time before telling me your splendid news, right?"

My voice is bitter and Jude's eyes slash with the hurt I just hurled at him. "Aria, don't be a child. I missed you and wanted to show you how much I thought about you while I was in London."

"Well, I guess there will be a lot of that in our future, huh? The thinking about the distance?"

Our voices are raising now, and there is no way Dad doesn't know something is going on up here. I pray he'll let it go once Jude eventually leaves because I know after this I won't be able to talk about what was going to happen.

I have to get Jude away from me. I can't go through one more person smashing my heart to pieces, so I'll smash his first in hopes that it will keep mine intact.

"I get it. You're doing what you have to to succeed. We both knew this wasn't ... it was convenient. Both being at Rogue, Clavering is hard up for any real dating opportunities."

As I say the words, it's as if my heart is being pulled out of my throat with them.

"Aria ..." Jude shoots me a look of sympathy as if his goal to make it to London also means my disappointment.

That's the thing though, it's sympathetic, not empathetic. He feels sad for me, not for leaving me. It doesn't seem as if he feels any upset at having to walk out on whatever it is that we've started here.

"You were always meant to go to London, we've just been ignoring that fact. You'll be brilliant, and soon enough, you won't even remember the small town of Clavering."

"Aria ..."

I cut Jude off again. "So just, go pack your bags! I'm sure they want you there for the match, straightaway. You'll be in the starting lineup this weekend—"

"Aria!" Jude bellows, the muscles in his neck and jaw tightening.

"No!" My rebuttal is more forceful. "No. I don't want to hear whatever it is you're going to say because I can't have your voice in my head telling me whatever it is. I don't want to know how much you care, or how you wish you didn't have to leave. I don't want to hear all the lame, cliché excuses people give when they walk out on someone else and don't want that person to be too crushed. Believe me, I know what it's like. So don't say them, Jude, because I can't listen to the echoes of your goodbyes resounding in my head for the next however much time."

"Would you—"

The only way I'll get through this is if I keep cutting him off. "Don't you dare. Jude, don't you dare ask me to come with you to London. You know I can't do that, and you know it will only break my heart more."

But he is already breaking my heart, in ways he should have known. The most detrimental thing that has ever happened to me, that has ruined my self-esteem and my worth and the chance at regular, healthy love, was my mother leaving us. Abandoning my father and me to pursue bigger dreams.

And right now, Jude is doing the exact same thing.

I've always suspected that, in the end, we would be ruined dramatically, in the fashion of a firework exploding. Jude would cheat on me, or his partying ways would be too much, or my inability to give time or affection would cause him to blow up in spectacular fashion.

This is so much worse. The slow conclusion, the grinding to a halt of our relationship ... it guts me worse than any sudden parting could have. I knew it was coming, that impact was bound to happen, and still, I chose to ignore it. We imploded at a snail's pace, in the weeks and days leading up to this.

I would never ask him not to go, this is his destiny, after all.

But some irrational part of my brain feels like I am ten years old all over again, being abandoned by the person I'd come to love the most.

"So we should end it." His voice is stone cold as he glares at me, the walls in his green eyes going up.

"I don't see any other way." We can't do long distance, our lives will be too different.

"Great. Then it's done." Jude drops the guillotine over my heart, and I feel it cleave in two.

There's nothing more to say, so he walks out. In an instant, the future I never wanted to hope for has just been pulled out from under me.

This is why I never allowed hope in. It's why I've never let it light up my heart again.

32

JUDE

London is its usual dreary, foggy self in my first few weeks of living here.

Which is fitting, as my mood isn't drastically different than the weather. My attitude matches the grey, sunless days and bitterly cold evenings. The flat Barry procured is a twenty-something bachelor's dream; complete with a sauna shower, retractable movie theater size screen in the living room, and a scotch slash wine room with perfectly attuned temperature settings. It's lavish and unnecessary, and I wonder more than once how Aria would make fun of me for moving in here.

I wonder all the time what Aria would say. We haven't spoken in the month since I left the academy and Clavering behind for good. And that's how long the organ in my chest has been weeping for.

I knew I'd gone about things all wrong. Going to her house, making her vulnerable about the place that she lived ... and then attacking her like she was my last meal. I suppose she was ...

Aria tempted me too much, and with how much I'd been

going back and forth, I had been like a one-minded fiend until I could get inside her. I should have told her before I'd shed her clothes that Rogue had finally called me up in a permanent capacity. That had been my fault, but what had happened next ... well, I can't take all the blame.

The girl I love ... she was petrified of her feelings for me. I saw it the moment I told her about London. Those walls had come up, she'd shut down, and in turn, put a firing squad in front of her heart if I even dared to get near it.

Aria is too scared to admit that she loves me, but I am a coward for not telling her, too. We are both bloody fools, and now, I am alone and sulking like a dog that has been kicked one too many times.

Today's match had been abysmal. A three to two loss that I'd been the deciding factor in, and I have a feeling all of London will be calling me a flop tomorrow.

I learned a long time ago never to blame one player for a loss because a squad has many chances to win a game. However, the penalty kick I missed contributed greatly. I never miss a shot like that, and it was bloody fate not on my side this time that I overshot the net.

No one in London is close enough to me to know how to comfort me. If Kingston and Vance were here, they'd suggest a round of FIFA or a couple of beers in our dorm room. Or a prank to cheer me up. If Aria were here, I could bury myself in her and forget about the shite day I'd had.

But I burned that bridge ... and my heart along with it. And my mates are still at the academy. So drowning my sorrows in a pint, alone, is my best option.

The Bock Club is a high-end gentlemen's pub frequented by British actors, artists, businessmen, and athletes. There's a waitlist to be accepted as a member, which I bypassed a year ago when the owners decided they wanted to extend membership to England's future football star.

I didn't feel like a crowded nightclub, there was no need for half-naked birds; a leather armchair in a quiet corner seemed the best company for my mood. So I head to the club, ask for a table in a private alcove, and the staff sets me up with an expensive bottle and lets me go to town.

My third glass is on the way to being finished when I see Franc Nasri walk in with his bloody band of tossers. Praying he'll leave me be, I scoot back in my chair more as they crowd up to the bar of the back room I'm currently occupying.

Nasri is France's number one goal-scorer, and a total twit. He is technically bereft, with sloppy footwork and a penchant for dirty tricks. The refs always happen to be looking the other way when he elbows someone in the throat or stomps on their boot.

The group orders their drinks, and I busy myself trying to think of the best way to slink out of here. I don't want to speak to anyone, especially Nasri, right now.

"Ah, if it isn't the loser of today's match." Nasri turns with a sneer on his face directed right at me.

My plan of escape is quickly thwarted and with just that simple sentence from the Frenchman, I feel my jaw click with fury.

I tip my head to him, trying to keep my tongue in check … which is hard after three tumblers full of alcohol. "Nasri, what a pleasure to see you. Didn't realize they let rats in here. Perhaps I need to think about that when it comes time to renew my membership."

Well, that wasn't holding my tongue.

His smirk falters when he realizes some of his friends are laughing at my mocking of him. "Didn't realize they let amateurs in here either. Or do we need to count the days since Niles finally brought you up from that peasant town?"

This wanker isn't worth it, I know that. He's jealous of me and trying to act like the king in front of his friends. But I'm in a foul mood and primed to unleash my frustration on someone, and he seems to be the prime target.

I know he's the best option I have when he lets the next couple of words tumble out of his mouth.

"Perhaps you need to up your caliber of women. That impoverished, bland girl you've been photographed with doesn't seem to be loosening your joints well enough."

"What did you say?" I set down the glass in an eerily calm manner.

The rat's French accent is painted with spittle from his thin lips. "I said, if you weren't so busy shagging average girls, you might have a better chance of scoring goals on the actual pitch."

Rage begins to brew in my veins, hot and lethal as his group of friends titter behind him. I am going to rip this guy apart limb by limb.

No one is here to stop me. I am alone, and in the heat of the moment, everything I've worked so hard on personally goes out the window. It doesn't matter that I have reformed myself into a better man, one worthy of Aria. She isn't here, she's thrown us away as easily as could be ... because she's scared. I'm not enough to make her brave enough to pursue what we had together, but I'm not going to let someone speak about her in this way.

I must blackout as I stand from my wingback chair and launch myself across the room at Nasri because the next couple of minutes are a blur of consciousness. My solid mass hits his and we wrestle to the floor, a flash of my fist sinking into his jaw, the whiz of his elbow catching me in the temple. Blood and screams and the cathartic feel of pain leaking out of my body and into my victim.

All too suddenly, someone is pulling me off a limp and

sobbing Nasri, yelling something into my face that I can't quite comprehend. He may have popped my eardrum, or maybe I'm in shock.

It doesn't dawn on me until later that I've just flushed my entire life down the drain.

33

ARIA

Having a taste of the champagne life is dangerous.

Because when you don't belong there and know the entire time you're in that moment that you'll need to go back to paying bills and living below the poverty line, it feels even worse when the rug is pulled out from under you.

I've experienced what it's like to travel first class or go to posh nightclubs. I've known what it means to stay in a penthouse and not worry about how much a limo cost. The food, the clothes, the glamour of it all was enticing.

And now, it's gone.

That isn't what has me in the dreariest of moods. No, they can take all that from me and I wouldn't bat an eyelash. While it was nice to experience, I've subsisted on far worse and I'll do it again.

What I don't think I'll be able to survive is the crushing ache of something breaking in my chest every bloody second. Jude left, fled like he hadn't been given enough time to leave everything he wanted to push out of his life behind. And I am stuck here, in Clavering, in the same old life that has been oppressing me for two years.

I am a survivor, yes, but ask me to survive in a world that has been brightened by the most unexpected boy imaginable, and it is bloody impossible. In every corner of every academy building, I feel him. It's as if my senses are overcome with the scent of Jude, my eyes play tricks on me as other boys walk across the academy pathways and I do a double take to see if it was really Jude.

The tunnels are off limits ... I can't handle venturing back to the spot where so many of our secret moments were had. And avoiding Kingston and Vance is a top priority.

In my life, I've never experienced this kind of sharp, yearning loss. Not even with my mother, who was biologically inclined to love me. Jude has opened my eyes to what the world could be, he's shown me excitement and freedom. Not only have I fallen in love with the man, something I never told him and now never would, but I've fallen in love with the kind of life he created for me. One where I wasn't downtrodden, or sad, or lonely all the time.

Having that taken away ... it does something to the essential makeup of a person.

The only thing that makes me feel slightly better? Well, not better, but maybe in good company with my misery, is the fact that Jude's bloody face was splashed all over the papers. Scratch that, it doesn't make me feel good at all. He'd gotten into a pub brawl with some French national team player who'd been taunting him.

I was severely disappointed, but maybe this was who Jude has always been. Never attempt to change the bad boy, because it will never work.

Patricia and Louisa must know something is up but by the grace of God, don't call attention to it. Perhaps, these days, I give off more of a dismal attitude and they know well enough to leave it alone.

Sitting at my station in the sew house, I'm trying to focus my attention fully on the kit I'm embroidering when Patricia comes by and leans a hip into the table.

"Aria, love, someone from the headmaster's office just rang. He wants to see you on the double."

My head shoots up because I have never been called in about anything. Not only am I a model worker, but Patricia is my direct boss. The only two times there has ever been a problem—a mishandled stitch and the time I'd been five minutes late because Dad had thrown up on my blouse—she had been the one to handle talking to me about them.

The organ in my chest, the one Jude shattered when he'd left, pounds against the cage of my ribs with nervous fear. Being called to Headmaster Darnot's office is like being called to the principal's office ... quite literally. I have no idea what I've done, and as Louisa and Patricia stare at me, I begin to wrack my brain for any indiscretion I could have committed.

Taking my lunch in the tunnels? There's no way they could care much about that. Had I sewn one of the kits wrong? Left a light on after I cleaned a certain part of the buildings?

I'm not sure, but whatever it is ... it's not a good sign that the headmaster wants to see me.

My body is sluggish as it rises from the stool I've been occupying for hours. I keep my mouth glued shut as I walk out of the sew house, my mind racing as my hands begin to sweat.

No amount of wiping them on my khaki pants as I walk disjointedly across the grounds can get them to dry.

As I walk into the headmaster's wing of one of the administrative buildings, and into the waiting area outside his office, the secretary gives me a curt nod. Does she know why I'm here? Perhaps I should ask her ...

No, even if she knows, she'll never tell me. From what I can remember, she's served Headmaster Darnot faithfully for over three decades.

A beep comes over the phone on her desk, she picks it up, nods into the receiver, and places it back down.

"You may go in," she says to me in a clipped tone.

I'm ushered into the headmaster's office, a place I've only been to when no one else is in the building. His desk comes into view first, the gleaming wood of it polished by me the night before. I wonder if he realizes that?

"Miss Lloyd, have a seat." Headmaster Darnot's hawk-like gaze flits over me, and I feel instantly vulnerable.

The man has a Napoleon-complex if I ever heard of one. The academy players loathe him, and it's said that he acts so harshly with the young men here because he has no real power in the grand scheme of the organization. Luckily, I've never had to have a genuine interaction with him ... until now.

I try to keep my voice calm and professional as I attempt to seek out why I might have been called in here. "Sir, have I done something wrong? I arrive promptly for all of my shifts, if there is something with the janitorial work you'd like done differently—"

"We're going to have to let you go, Miss Lloyd." He looks me straight in the face with his emotionless eyes.

I must look like a fish because my mouth simply won't stop gaping open. "I'm ... I'm sorry, what?"

"The academy is relieving you of your position. Seeing as how your boyfriend just caused a rather enormous mess for the club, we decided it was best to rid ourselves of any ... baggage he left in his wake."

Realization dawns on me, and confusion sets in at almost the same time. "I'm being shown the door because Jude Davies got into some pub brawl in London? I'm not quite sure what that has to do with me. And we are no longer dating, so it shouldn't be an issue. I swear to you, Headmaster, I am not in contact with him."

My voice takes on a pleading edge at the end of my sentence, but I can see that none of my explanations have affected him in the slightest. Darnot looks down his nose at me, and his mouth flicks up in a sneer.

"That may be a technicality, but we're scrubbing this academy of any stain of Jude Davies, and unfortunately, you're collateral damage. You'll turn in your keys and passes to the campus by end of day, and any training materials for your protégé should be left with Patricia."

My lungs begin to seize, and my body is throttled into panic mode. "Headmaster, please, I need this job. I swear, I have always been a top-notch employee, I'll work longer shifts, I'll ... please, you don't understand ..."

Emotion catches in my throat as I try to blink back the tears threatening to fall. I can see it all *so* clearly, the crumbling pieces of my world falling from the sky and burning to ash as they touch the ground. This job, it's more than essential. Without money, without work, I can' help my father. We can't eat, we'll be evicted ...

"Unfortunately, Miss Lloyd, you shouldn't have let your foolish female intuitions get in the way. This is your problem now, and there is nothing more I can do. Next time, perhaps don't hitch your wagon to a wild one."

With a flick of his wrist, he shoos me from his office, dismissing me like some kind of guttersnipe. I want to plead more, to get down on my knees and beg, but I can feel the smug satisfaction coming off the headmaster in waves ... and I know there is nothing more I can say.

I've known from the beginning that falling into bed with Jude, for lack of better terms, was going to end terribly. That associating with him would only cause me fatal harm, and I was correct. Not only have I lost my heart, but now I've lost the means to keep my family from falling fully into poverty.

Too numb to cry, too distraught to throw myself on the ground and scream at the gods, I walk out of his office and through the grounds, blind to anything else around me.

Because the only thing running through my mind is one question.

How will I save my father's life now?

34

ARIA

"Aria, I think something is wrong."

These are the words I'm greeted with as I walk into my house, and for a second, I wonder how my dad knows already that I've been sacked.

"Did someone from the school call you?" I ask from the tiny entryway as I shed my coat.

Walking into the living room, I'm greeted by the most horrific sight I've ever seen.

Dad is on his hands and knees, but in a haphazard way that looks like he must have fallen out of his chair. His limbs are rigid but bent at strange angles, and there is ...

Blood. Staining the carpet in ugly brown patches.

It's dripping from his mouth, covering his hands, and his eyes are so wide and pale that I think he must see death lurking behind me.

"Dad?" I tremble, my entire body going into shock.

"I think something is wrong," he says as his voice breaks, and then passes out on the floor in front of me.

My system goes into panic mode, adrenaline coursing

through my veins and fueling me to do one thing and one thing only.

Save him.

I honestly don't remember calling the ambulance or opening the door for them when they showed up. The period of time from the point of him passing out to when I walked into the emergency room is an utter blur. All I can see, the memory seared into the frontal lobe of my brain, is the horrified panic on my father's face as I first took in the scene of the living room.

The doctors rush him off to somewhere in the hospital ... I'm too distressed to catch anything but bits and pieces of conversations being relayed to me. The nurse at the check-in desk hands me a clipboard and I stare at it.

"Miss? You need to fill out your father's information."

"Where have they taken him?" I can't focus, it's as if my mind has splintered into seven different pieces.

"He's going into surgery. After you fill out his information, we can have someone take you to the waiting room on the floor he'll be on," she explains, taking a bit of pity on me.

She probably sees half-dazed people like me every hour, coming in here with ill relatives. She probably holds the hands of plenty ... but right now, that person is me. And even though I'm the strong one, I'm the one our family of two leans on to be the rock, in this time of need, I find I can't pull it together.

I'm ninety percent sure I scribble down gibberish on the registration paperwork, but the nurse seems to approve it because fifteen minutes later, I'm being escorted to an elevator and finally deposited in a small waiting room with a door that closes.

I'm not sure if that's good or bad. You know, sometimes in movies or what not, they show the family of the about-to-be ... dead person in an offshoot waiting room instead of the main one. So that when they break down, it isn't in full view of every other person in the hospital.

My hands shake just thinking about this, and the fear that I might really lose my dad starts to creep in, paralyzing every nerve in my body. Time must be moving, but if it is, I can't feel it. It's as if I sit in this small, auxiliary waiting room alone for years, or maybe decades. No noise, no movement around me.

Finally, my head whips to the door as I hear the knob twist open, and a man in scrubs appears before me.

"Miss Lloyd? You're Edward's daughter?" He relays my father's first name and I nod. "Your father is stable. Still in surgery, but stable."

"Is he ... will he ..." I can't say the words that have been flashing through my head since I found him in a puddle of his own blood.

The doctor blanches and gives me a sympathetic smile. "He's going to be okay. We found a ruptured ulcer in his stomach ... the inflammation was likely caused by the chemotherapy treatments he's been undergoing. The bleeding was a result of the ulcer, but we have it under control now and are just trying to clean it out. He'll be in recovery in about an hour or so."

Sucking in lungfuls of deep breaths, I press my palm to my chest to calm my rattled heart. *He's going to be okay* ... I just have to keep repeating it to myself over and over again.

"Can you give me the name of his oncologist and general doctors? I'd like to touch base with them," the doctor says.

I give him all the information he's asking about, and he leaves me with another assurance that Dad will be okay coming out of surgery. Notice how he doesn't say *just fine*, because we both know the man is fighting cancer and there are no guarantees when it comes to that.

A half an hour after he leaves, my phone rings. I don't even realize where it's coming from at first, because I rarely get calls to the thing. And now, with no job, no boyfriend and the only person close to me in surgery, it's bizarre I'd be receiving a ring from anyone.

"Hello?" My voice sounds ragged and tired.

"Hi, Aria, it's Ian Rethal. How are you getting on? Listen, the demo is going to be played on a radio station later this week, and there is an executive at my label who thinks it's bloody brilliant."

At any other moment, I'd be elated. I'd be jumping up and down and letting the euphoric rush of good luck suffuse my body. But right now, I can do little more than tell Ian, "Wonderful."

Silence on the other end. "Aria, did you hear me? Your song is going to be played on the radio! And once it gets some circulation, and I can get it on some streaming services, you'll be cut a check from the royalties!"

The mention of money gets my blood pumping a bit. "That will be a welcome thing. Sorry, Ian ... it's not a great time. My father was rushed to hospital this morning and I can't ... I'm glad to hear the news. But I have other things on my plate right now."

"Oh, Aria, I apologize ... I know it isn't a great time, but we'd like to have you do an interview with a reporter in anticipation of the single. Can he give you a call tomorrow?"

I have no idea what the rest of my week will hold. My father is still fighting for his life. "Ian, I won't be able to do that."

"Aria, you know this is the chance a million singers would jump at ..." He probably thinks I'm mental.

I nod into the phone, though he can't see me. "And right now, I'm not one of them. There are more important things. Thank you for letting me know about the radio, Ian. I hope the song does well."

I disconnect the call before he can spit any more industry talk at me. What a shame, that the moment something goes right for me, I can't even recognize how big of a deal it is. Once again, my universe has robbed me of any personal joy. Not that I care ... the only thing I can think about is getting into that recovery room to give my dad a hug. To make sure that he is, in fact, going to be okay.

My thoughts need a distraction, and I pick up the closest issue of Daily Mail on the table next to me. As if the world hasn't taunted me enough today, lo and behold, there is Jude Davies' gorgeous mug on the cover.

And I do mean mugshot. Even with a bloody nose and a split lip, up against the brick police station wall, he's still the most dishy man I've ever laid eyes on. The criminal photo only makes him appear more dangerous, as if he could send a poison arrow through your heart with one look.

The headline beneath the photo reads, "The Prince of the Pitch off to Prison?"

I can't help it, I flip to the page number the cover story gives and read through the piece. It paints Jude as a constant cock up. Says he is arrogant and entitled. The writer claims that the future football legend cares nothing for anyone in his life and that he is a disappointment to the country. Words like *playboy*, *womanizer*, *brawler*, and *troublemaker* are used.

The article paints him in the worst light possible ... the author clearly doesn't know the real man behind this photo.

No matter how much I loathe Jude at this moment, no matter how he has broken my heart in a million ways, I can't get on board with this hack job.

I know the real Jude Davies, despite what the world thinks of him. Despite how he is trying to self-implode.

35

JUDE

A scraping noise jolts me from sleep, and I must sit up too quickly, because suddenly it feels like the entire world is tilting.

"*Jesus Christ* ..." I curse, steadying my hand on the bed.

My right eye is nearly swollen shut, and the pounding in my head threatens to explode. It wouldn't surprise me if, at any moment now, my brain matter were to splatter all over the nearest walls.

Speaking of the walls, and the bed ... they aren't mine. As I twist around, my torso screaming in pain while I do so, I'm met with antique furnishings and old tapestries hung on every available inch of wall. It's like I'm sitting in the middle of a *Game of Thrones* set or some shite.

A harsh knock sounds on the door. "Get up or you'll miss breakfast and we don't wait for daft blokes in this house."

Barry's voice comes through the wood, and I groan. Bloody hell, it's not enough that I took a literal beating, but now I'm apparently at Barry's house and will have to take a verbal lashing from him?

Walking into the hall, I glance around. I've only ever been to his house, one of those gigantic London brownstones in a posh neighborhood, once before. The whole place is decorated with a style akin to that of my grandmum, and the sound of children floats through the place.

Children? Since when does Barry have children?

Making my way toward the smell of beans and bacon, I find the kitchen ... and a family of four seated in it. Barry, his wife—whose name I forget—and two small primary-school aged boys. They're in uniforms with their hair combed slickly back, and his wife gives me a wry smile like she knows I'm about to get a proper lashing.

"Let's eat in my office," Barry says gruffly and picks up two plates, expecting me to follow.

I do, only because I have no idea what the hell is going on.

"How did I get here?" I ask once we're alone in the study with the door closed.

Barry places a napkin on his lap. "You got into that brawl with Nasri three days ago. After you were arrested and released, you went home and proceeded to drain every liquor bottle in your apartment. I found you passed out that evening around ten p.m. when I basically knocked your door down because I hadn't heard from you. I took you back here to make sure you didn't suffocate on your own vomit, or worse, make any other press mistakes. You've been asleep for almost twenty hours."

"*Christ ...*" I wipe a hand down my face, feeling ragged.

Barry tucks into his breakfast and doesn't look at me while addressing the situation. "To say I'm disappointed would be too obvious. You're my client and I'm paid to fix your mistakes, but, Jude ... you really cocked up this time. And you were doing so well. While I do damage control, you have a sit down with Niles at noon today. So best eat that breakfast and then shower, because there is a nine in ten chance he'll make the decision to sell you. You better put your bloody charm on today, chap."

"He said something about Aria," I deadpan.

"Who, Niles?" Barry's eyes are full of confusion.

I look away, not even able to stomach the thought of breakfast right now. "Nasri. At the club, he started talking shite about me dating average birds. I lost it. I already miss her so much ..."

The emotion steals my voice in a way I never thought possible, and I have to swallow against tears. My life is on the brink of disaster, and the only thing I care about is defending Aria's honor. The only thing I can think about is how she's not here right now, and that when she finds out what I've done, she'll think the worst of me.

Barry sighs, setting his fork down. "Mate, I wasn't going to tell you this ... but I think it's necessary. It'll be the kick in the ass you need on the pitch, but also to grow up and tell the girl you love her. Long distance isn't the end of the world, you know. My wife and I did it for two years before we were married. You're a fool for leaving Clavering and not telling Aria how you feel."

My skin suddenly feels two sizes too small. "Tell me what?"

"Once the academy heard about the brawl, or Headmaster Darnot more specifically, he ... he used it to give Aria the sack. I got the call from them two days ago that she's been relieved of her duties. And then I got a call from Ian Rethal yesterday, the music label bloke. Seems he couldn't get a hold of you and wanted me to try to convince you to convince Aria to give an interview. Said she refused because her father is in hospital, but that the interview would help launch her new single. This Ian fellow seemed in a panic, like if she didn't talk to this reporter, the song might flop."

Barry keeps speaking, but I haven't heard anything past "her father is in hospital."

"Aria's father is in hospital? And she was sacked because of me?" My heart, what is left of it, goes up in a puff of smoke.

This is all, every single bit of it, my fault. Her father is ill, hanging in the balance if Aria was so distracted that she wouldn't take a phone call from Ian about an opportunity that could change her life. The hairs on the back of my neck stand up, and bile begins to rise in my throat.

I'd finally caused the ultimate downfall, and it wasn't even to myself. Aria's job at the academy is everything to her. It means her family can live another day, that she can provide food and shelter to her ailing father. It's close to home, so she can access the campus without a car and can go home over lunch to check on Edward. My delinquent behavior has robbed her of the very thing she needs most.

"You need to ... I need to ..." My thoughts are scattered between figuring out how to help Aria, talk to Niles, do damage control on my career, and be with her while her father fights through illness.

Barry seems to understand and sets a calm hand on my shaking one. "I have already been in touch with Aria's loan officers, and I've pulled from your accounts to cover their monthly expenses for the next year. Don't ask me how I did it, you're not privy to know nor do we want to anger anyone more than necessary when Aria, the stubborn girl, finds out you've paid all of her bills and then some. But it's already done, so she won't be able to argue too much. Next, you need to go talk to Niles. Tell him everything. I will take care of the press, your reputation, and having the charges dropped once I tell the police Nasri instigated it. I have some dirt I've dug up that will convince him pressing charges isn't the right way to handle this. The most important thing right now is cementing your place on the pitch, and then you can go to Aria. Focus, Jude. Do you understand?"

I knew I employed Barry for a reason. Just his simple instructions seem to bring a dead calm over me, smoothing out the chaos that was about to erupt in my chest.

There's one chance to get this all right, and if by some stroke of luck it works, I'll have everything I ever wanted.

36

JUDE

"You're ... early."

Niles pauses as he walks into his office, visible shock on his face as he takes in the image of me sitting ramrod straight in a chair opposite his on the other side of the desk.

"I can take direction. And I know that you say on time is ten minutes late, so."

"I do say that." He sighs as he sits down in his leather high-back chair. "You fucked up, Jude. Again."

"I did." I nod in agreement.

Niles Harrington raises an eyebrow. "No if, ands, or buts? No excuses? Well, I can say I expected this conversation to take a very different tone."

Shrugging, I look my coach right in the eye. "Those things would do me no good. I fucked up, as you said. It's been the last of a long line of cock-ups, and I do mean the last. I won't sit here and tell you the reason I beat his face to a pulp, although it was a justified one. I'm not sorry I did it ... but I am apologetic that it was at the expense of the Bock Club and that it embarrasses RFC. I understand that there are going to be consequences, but I wanted to tell you that if you extend me one more chance, I will never besmirch the Rogue name again. I came to London on a mission, leaving everything I love and know behind to fulfill my potential and win you trophies. It's what I've always wanted since I was a boy."

"And yet, you've continued to laugh in the face of rules and cause havoc left and right." Niles jaw clicks, and I know he's getting angrier by the second.

"I was a reckless youth, I admit that. I'm still young and learning how to be the role model I need to be to those young fans. I won't sit here and wax romantic ... you know there is a girl in my life. Committing to her has grounded me. And before that, I cared for my brothers as the lone adult and authority figure in their immediate family. I've taken on far more responsibility than a lot of your adult players, at a time when I couldn't even legally walk into a pub and order a pint. Struggling with the weight of that duty, growing up in the public eye with so much expectation, it would be tough for anyone. Aria, my girl ... she's shown me that I don't get to use those excuses anymore. That I'm here, I'm grown, and it's time to start acting like it. She sure as bloody hell does. I may be spitting out my shite at you, but I want you to understand where I'm coming from. And why I deserve to stay at Rogue Football Club. Moving forward, I'll be the model player."

He regards me for a second as I suck in a breath. The diatribe was not only vocally exhausting but mentally.

"I've given you a lot of chances, Jude. When you were first signed to the academy, I was impressed at the talent in such a young child. As you grew, you kept proving that your style of play was going to be unmatched when the full extent of it could be unfurled on the pitch. In your first match in the stadium here in London, I was floored by your ability. The type of player you are only comes around ... maybe once or twice in a lifetime. I had Killian talk to you a while back because he understands where you sit. He knows the pressure his talent puts on him, how it makes the world look at him. And he also knows what it's like to fuck up and have to deal with the heartbreak that life and scandal bring."

I hang on his words, my heart threatening to burst from my chest. And any moment, he can drop the anvil over my head and end my career in London as I know it.

"One more chance, Davies. Because you're too bloody talented for me to let you go without exhausting every option. And ... I think you're a stand-up guy, at the heart of it. Show the world the man who confessed all of that to me, and maybe I won't ride your arse as much."

Yeah, right, he gets off on using scare tactics on his players. But I'm not about to argue.

"Thank you, sir. Truly, you don't know how grateful I am."

Niles waves me off. "Yeah, yeah ... now go suit up, we have to beat Milligan today or I may reconsider how lenient I'm being."

Now I clear my throat. "I appreciate everything you've done for me. And I know I just testified that I would never let you down again ... but I have to ask for one more favor."

I try not to let my voice waver.

"What?" Harrington looks down his nose at me.

"My girlfriend's father is in the hospital. He's fighting cancer, and I'd like to be there for her."

"We have a match today," he points out.

"Yes, we do ... but family is more important. If there is anything I've learned over all of my mistakes and lessons through the years is that there is nothing above family."

Niles points at me. "That is the kind of answer I can respect. Now go, before I change my mind. I expect you back here in a week, completely ready to annihilate our opponent."

He doesn't have to tell me twice, on any of the fronts.

37

ARIA

Dad seems groggy when he wakes up today.

Sometimes, the nurse told me, patients can feel good in the hours directly after surgery, and those feelings can even bleed into day one post-operation. It's the days or even weeks after that can be the toughest.

I see that now, on the start of day three in the hospital. He's irritable, in pain, has no appetite and doesn't want me fussing over him. This scares me, although the staff here have made it perfectly clear he's going to recover nicely from the ruptured ulcer. But, as always, I'm a bundle of unspoken panic. The tears that have been trapped in my chest ever since I walked into his hospital room feel like they're searing me from the inside out. I can't break down in front of Dad, I'm supposed to be the strong one.

Unfortunately, in the rush to leave for the hospital, the only things I grabbed were my house keys and mobile. The crappy laptop, a change of clothes, Dad's favorite slippers ... they were all at home. I haven't showered in two days, and I know I have to log onto the computer to pay this month's bills. One was due yesterday, and the others at the end of this week.

Not that it matters … I don't have enough money to pay them anyway. The last paycheck from Rogue Academy won't come until next week, and with no overtime, it will be less than half of what we need to keep the lights on. My nerves tense and my heart beats in an unsteady fashion any time I try to figure out how we're going to survive now.

"Aria, will you stop it!" Dad snaps at me as I try to fluff his pillows for the third time in an hour.

I pull my hands back as if he's burned me. "I'm just trying to take care of you."

"I'm the parent, you're the child. I'm supposed to be taking care of you!" His voice takes on a frustrated note, and I can tell he either needs to sleep or another dose of pain meds.

"I'm going to go find the nurse." Ignoring his need to try to cut me down, I walk into the hall in search of some relief for Dad.

And bump straight into a person who looks so out of place in a Clavering hospital, he might as well be a mystical unicorn.

"Hi," Jude says, steadying me as I barrel into him.

Everything goes still for a moment as I look into his perfectly magnificent face. He's here, holding me up, looking at me in a way that has tears pooling in my eyes.

"What are you doing here?" My voice breaks on a sob but I rein it in and move out of his gentle grip.

My voice must be too loud, or those around us are starting to notice Jude Davies standing in the middle of the hospital because he steps into me and turns us quickly down the hall and slips into the first empty waiting room he sees.

"How is your dad? Is it the cancer, has it progressed?" Jude asks first thing when I step into the room behind him.

The anger, the one that overrules the heartbreak he caused, surfaces in bubbling, furious emotions. "What the hell are you doing here, Jude? You have no right to come here, to … to what?

Act like some knight ready to save my kingdom from burning to the ground?"

I don't need him to come to my rescue. He left without a backward glance ... we haven't spoken in a month and a half. Off he'd gone to London, to fulfill his destiny without so much as a consideration into how deeply I feel for him. This isn't the time to play the hero, and I won't let him. My stubborn pride, and my shattered love, will not allow Jude Davies to get the best of them ever again.

But, it appears Jude is going to fight just as hard as I am. "Maybe I am! Would that be so horrible of me, Aria? To care about you enough to come running when your world is hanging in the balance? I cocked this all up before, it doesn't mean I can't correct it! I came here to see how your father is doing, to lend you a shoulder to lean on in troubled times, and to tell you that I am so in love with you that I'll gladly stand here fighting with your pigheaded ego because I even love that part of you!"

I physically falter, visibly stutter where I stand as those three very big words come out of his mouth. "You ... what?"

Perhaps I'm in shock because I can't even form a sentence, much less a thought. Looking back, I'll wonder if this was a tactic of Jude's to stun me so much that he just collected his prize and won me over easily. It wouldn't be a surprise, given his talent for catching his opponent off guard.

"I love you. It's that simple, and that complicated. I never should have left Clavering without telling you, and I never should have let you push me away. You're so strong, Aria. You balance the world on your shoulders and bare your teeth at anything or anyone that threatens your independent struggling. I'm not going to let you do that anymore ... and I'm not going to be frightened of how I feel any longer. I'm a grown-up, and since the day I met you, I've slowly realized that I need to start acting like one. So, yes, I'm going to be here for you. To check on how not only your dad is doing, but how you're holding up. I'm going to make sure you both have everything you need, and you can try to bang your chest and make me leave. I'm not going anywhere."

Now I crack, coming apart at the seams as Jude scoops me into his arms. Ugly cries, the kind that shakes my core and causes me to use his shirt as a tissue, break free from my throat. Everything comes out; the fear about my father, the relief that Jude came back for me, the knowledge that he loves me just as much as I love him ... it all drowns me like a tidal wave.

"The academy, they sacked me ..." I hiccup.

He rubs my back in slow, gentle circles. "I'm going to take care of everything. No arguing about that."

Right now, I couldn't if I tried. Having someone to lean on, being strong enough inside to allow this man who loves me to be the one I lean on ... we've both come a long way. But something is keeping me from saying it back, no matter how deeply I feel it in my heart.

Perhaps it's the fact that the only other person I love is lying just feet from here, fighting for his life. Telling someone else that I love them when my biggest love might be taken away, is terribly daunting.

Sensing the need to break the tension within me, Jude speaks.

"Now, can I go visit with your dad? You think I only came here for you? Sheesh, woman ..." Jude mocks, wrapping me in an embrace that opposes his sarcastic comment.

By the time we make it back to my father's hospital room, the nurse tells us that he's had another round of pain medication and will probably be sleeping for a while.

I fill Jude in on what happened with Darnot and then finding my father in our living room. He almost punches the wall, he's that angry at his former headmaster. A couple of highly defamatory curses slip past his lips, and I have to wrap my arms around him to get him to stop.

We talk about London, about why he got into a brawl with the French player. The shock I feel from hearing that he was defending my honor is both surprising, but satisfactory. I tell Jude that while I appreciate his standing up for me, I don't need him to do it when it lands him in the doghouse with Niles Harrington.

He goes on to tell me about their talk before he drove to Clavering and says that he never wants to be apart from me again.

Me? I can't think about all that right now. I want to be together again, but I also know that I won't have any clarity on other situations until I know what Dad's fate is.

A little time passes, and Dad's oncologist walks into the room. I grab Jude's hand for support. He squeezes back, and just the warmth of his skin on mine makes me feel better.

"Oh, I didn't realize he was sleeping, I can come back." Dr. Bradley observes my father in the bed and turns to leave.

"No, please don't. Can you ... can you give me the update? You see, I haven't heard much about his progress or lack thereof, and ..." I trail off, not able to continue.

If he isn't getting better, I'm not sure I'm strong enough to withstand watching him lose this battle.

Dr. Bradley looks at Jude, his expression unsure, and then his face resolves itself. He probably knows I won't leave him alone until he gives me an update.

"I asked the staff here to do some bloodwork and scans. We had the lab push the job through, and while he still isn't in remission ... his counts are up and the tumor has shrunken to the point where we'll be able to go in and get all of it. I'm pretty confident about that. The surgery won't be until this round of radiation is done, but it's looking really promising."

The tears that started with Jude's confession begin again and won't stop. They cloud my vision, and the lightness I feel threatens to bring me to my knees. It's dizzying, being light as a feather when you've felt weight bearing down on you for so long.

"It was the last of the chemo fighting off the bad cells. He's almost in the clear, Aria." Dad's oncologist pats me on the shoulder and then leaves the room.

Finally, I let it trickle in. That feeling I've held at bay for so long, for years even.

Hope, strong as the tide of the ocean, washes over me. It seems that the things I dared not pray for might actually be coming true.

38

JUDE

Two days later, Edward is discharged from the hospital and we bring him home.

Aria had been living by his bedside at the hospital, even though her father and I both insisted she let me take her back to their house to shower and sleep. But, in usual stubborn fashion, my girl refused. So, I spent every second with her next to his bedside.

And now, I've spent the last couple of hours under their roof, with no intention of leaving. I have three more days here, and I am going to make the most of them. Starting with helping Aria focus on her next move, now that we know her father is on the mend.

We lie in her tiny twin bed, the door to her room open so she can hear her dad call if he needs her assistance.

She jolts halfway up, struggling out of my embrace. "Oh, the sewer bill, I completely forgot—"

"It's taken care of, love." I pull her back to me, nestling her in the crook of my arm and planting a kiss on her forehead.

"I will make it up to you, pay you back." Aria's voice sounds apologetic.

Putting a finger to her lips, I silence her. "You'll do no such thing. It's a miracle I didn't force you to take my help from the moment I met you, so now I'm just catching up. The best way to repay me? Do the interview, love. Forget all the madness occupying your head right now and talk to the reporter about the beautiful voice you've been given."

Her hazel, gold-flecked eyes meet mine. "I'm ... scared."

My thumb caresses her cheek. "Eh, just picture everyone naked, love."

Aria chuckles. "I already do that when I'm with you, constantly. Plus, don't tell me you're picturing other people naked."

"Just you." I give her a devilish gleam.

She seems to fixate on a speck of yarn on my shirt and picks at it for a few seconds. "All right, I'll do the interview."

Sitting up, she's jostled as I reach for my phone. "Great, I'll tell Barry you're ready now."

"What?" Aria's voice is sheer panic. "Can't we at least wait until tomorrow?"

"Nope, you'll chicken out," I say as the phone rings through to Barry.

For the time being, we all agree it's for the best if he represents her interests moving forward. I trust Barry, which means Aria trusts him because she values my judgment. If she has a professional handling her calls and interviews from the beginning, she'll be that much better off.

"Yeah, she's ready." I don't even bother saying hi.

Hanging up when Barry says he'll set it up right now, I turn to see Aria gaping at me.

"Do things in your world always move this fast? I'm not sure I want to be a part of this lifestyle ..." Her voice is small and meek.

"Love, the sooner you realize you're stronger than any person

I've ever met in *my* world, the sooner you'll know that you can make *your* world whatever you want it to be."

And she can. If she wants to take things slow, never do interviews, only sing for small venues ... whatever it is, Aria can make it so. She is so talented, no one is going to say no to her. And she has thicker skin than any person I have ever encountered.

Her cell phone begins to ring, and she jumps at the sound.

"That'll be the reporter," I tell her, glad that Barry worked so quickly. I didn't want to give Aria time to change her mind.

"Will you stay with me? Through the interview?" Aria grabs my hand as I stand to leave.

"This is your time to shine," I tell her.

"But you've done this before. I want someone on my side who has experience in this arena, just to make sure that I don't stick my foot in my mouth. Plus ... you're just nice to look at." Aria waggles her eyebrows at me.

I nod, and motion for her to pick it up before the call drops.

"Hello?" Aria greets the caller. "Yes, this is she. Thank you for giving me a call on short notice."

My girl puts her finger to her lips, to tell me to stay quiet, and then puts the call on speaker.

"Of course. This is Megan Gilbert with *Today's Tea*. I wanted to ask you a few questions about your upcoming single."

I'm familiar with Megan and her publication. Part newsworthy, part gossip column, the outlet is a reputable one with just enough scandal to keep its readers entertained.

And Megan is a solid writer which is the only reason Barry and I agreed with Ian to let Aria do the interview. Not that I am trying to control her career in any way, but I know how the media can turn stories. I'm not going to let that happen so early on to the woman I love.

"Great." Aria awaits her first question.

"So, before we jump into the music, which Ian sent me and I

think has a great vibe, let me ask you; do you think that Jude Davies has gone off the rail since your breakup?"

We're both dead silent for a minute, and I can see the annoyance evident on her beautiful face as Aria grinds her teeth. How the hell did Megan even get word that we'd broken up? Or that we were ever an item? Sure people got pictures of us in London or the occasional photog who came to Clavering caught us walking ... but we've never said a thing to the press. And we hadn't said anything when I left for London and we'd been broken up for a month.

"I will give no more answers to your interview questions unless you swear to print this next one word for word, got it?" Her tone is ice cold.

"I understand," Megan Gilbert says solemnly.

"Jude Davies is the most loyal, and strongest person I've ever met. His soul is good to its core, and the things being printed about him right now, about his quick reactions or temper, are dead wrong. Jude is kind, fair, and supportive ... he is one of the best men I've ever had the pleasure to know. The media's perception of him, and how they spread it to the people, tarnishes all the high-quality aspects of his persona. Sure, he is human, as we all are. But he's grown up in the public eye, had tremendous personal losses, and deals with everything around him in a logical way. Imagine if everything you did was magnified through a giant lens for the world to see?"

Aria finishes her calm tirade and looks to me, those hazel eyes shining with fierce loyalty and, if I dare to hope, love.

She hasn't said it back to me yet ... in two days she hasn't returned my sentiments. I'm not going to push it, but we both know I'm not a patient man when it comes to something I want. Soon, I'll have to pin her down and use my hands in the way she likes just to get her to admit she loves me.

"I think we can put that into print," Megan Gilbert clips out on the other end and I know my girl has schooled her.

This reporter thought she'd be getting easy prey, when in reality she's on a call with a quiet killer.

The rest of the interview goes swimmingly as Megan asks Aria about her music, where she wants her career to go, her favorite singers and what influences her. I hold her hand through it all, so proud that this kick-ass bird is the one I get to spend every day with. And, though she'll fight me every step of the way, the one I get to take care of. Because that's how I show my love ... she just told the reporter so.

"You did amazing." I lean over as she disconnects the call, gently taking her jaw in my hand and planting a soft kiss on her lips.

The caress of my mouth on hers lingers on, neither of us committing to more but not stopping. It's been so long since I've tasted her fully; since I've been inside her. My cock hardens with the knowledge that we're alone in her bedroom, even if Edward lies in a sickbed down the hall.

Pulling back, Aria looks me square in the eye. "I love you. As much as I tried not to fall for you, it was hopeless from the start. Loving you is as natural to me as breathing, and I'm not fighting it anymore."

And she's successfully stopped my heart. Makes it come to a full halt because no words have ever meant as much to me as hearing those ones from her. I never knew how much I needed her to say them, or how I've been waiting my entire life for this girl, this exact one, to tell me she is in love with me.

"Well, now that we've agreed on that, let me show you just how much I love you."

I stifle her giggle with my lips as I roll on top of her, testing out just how much force I can put into the bed without it squeaking.

39

ARIA

Walking into the family suite at the Rogue Football Club stadium brings an intense, sweeping feeling of déjà vu.

It was many months ago that I was escorted here as Jude Davies' handler the first time I ever spent the weekend with him in London. Now, it's a bi-weekly occurrence. He sends a car to Clavering on Friday, and I stay with him until Sunday, soaking up the alone time we have together.

And watching him play … it is one of my favorite things now. Jude's raw strength and power out on the pitch, it gives me goose bumps just sitting up here in the luxury box. The drive he exhibits, it makes me want to perfect my own craft. Sometimes, I have meetings with Ian on these weekend trips out to London, to talk about songwriting or sampling tracks some producer sent over.

Something I'd never counted on is how fast my demo took off. The first radio station that played it saw a good interest in it with their listeners. So another station picked it up, and pretty soon, social media users were posting it on their Instagram stories or sharing the YouTube audio to Facebook. I was shocked when Jude showed me his timeline, which featured two of his friends sharing *my* song.

It didn't feel real whatsoever, and after the interview I gave about my life and Jude, it seemed the popularity only increased. I don't want to say my *popularity*, because that sounds conceited and it ... is a bunch of bullshit. I'm still the same girl who lives in a dodgy row home in Clavering with her dad.

But, it's nice to get some recognition, and the check that Ian and the label mailed to me. Fifteen thousand pounds, and this is just the start of it. That kind of money will help us until I can record the full album and get it selling. The label wants to fast track that, an emotion-packed ten song album that I'll live in the studio to record as quickly as possible. I'm anxious, and a little nervous about how intense the work will be ... but I am ready.

The family suite is oddly empty today, with only a few people scattered about. Perhaps because it's a night match, and all the wives with little ones are home tucking them into bed.

I walk across the room, order myself a cup of tea from the bartender, and go to sit in my usual spot. The third table, pushed up to the glass so that I can have the best angle of Jude sprinting to the opposing team's goal. Except when I get there, my table is already taken.

By a woman whose face I've seen splashed all over every magazine.

"You're Leah Ramsey." I blink, starstruck.

You'd have to have lived under a rock for the last five years to not know who Killian Ramsey's wife is. I mean, her husband himself is the bloody king of English football ... the guy is a bigger rock star than Jude, and my cocky boyfriend will even admit that to you. But his wife? She is the real celebrity.

Leah runs her own public relations firm, is a mum to two kids, has perfect hair, organizes *loads* of charities and I heard she's best friends with Kate Middleton. If she isn't my hero, I'm not sure I have one then.

"God, and now I sound like a twit. I'm sorry ..." I begin to walk off to the other side of the room, shaking my head at myself, when her voice stops me.

"Wait, aren't you ... Aria? Jude's girlfriend, the one with the smashing voice?" Her American accent catches me off guard because it's almost as if Britain has adopted her as their own.

Holy bollocks, she knows who I am! "Um ... yes."

"Oh, I just love your song! Your voice is just beautiful," she compliments, and I'm already smitten with her. "But don't go calling yourself a twit, it only allows other people to do it. Sit with me?"

And now I love her even more. "Is ... is Killian, your husband, here, too?"

Is it weird to call her husband by his first name when I don't even know him? I feel like I do though, as does the whole country.

Leah rolls her eyes. "He's sitting down with the coaches. Seems that even in his retirement, I can't escape a soccer stadium. But, I guess it's nice to have a night away from the kids. As much as I love them, mama needs her wine and quiet time."

I have to swallow the chuckle at her calling the sport soccer. I'm sure Killian hates that. "It's probably nice to have time alone with your husband, too?"

"Savor this time you have with Jude. I didn't realize how much I'd miss it just being the two of us." I must twitch because she looks at me with a knowing smile. "Oh, I apologize for the forwardness. It's just ... I've been around a lot of players' wives over the years and my ability to read people has become almost *too* good. We're all the in the same boat, us wives, and I can tell you're one of the good ones. Those are rare to find in these family suites. Plus, I hear Killian blabber on about mentoring Jude at least four times a day, so I feel like I know you two."

It's hard to contain my admiration. "I'm … humbled. Gosh, I feel like I have a thousand questions I could ask you."

"Ask away. Let's both be honest, girl talk is way more interesting than this sport our men are always obsessing over." She smiles.

Her honesty makes me laugh. "Well, I guess the most relevant thing for me right now would be … how did you develop a thick skin when it came to your relationship?"

Leah nods sagely. "You don't, honestly. You just care enough about the man you love to ignore all the shit that people say about you. Can I give you some real advice? The answer to the question I wish you would have asked? Because apparently, that's what I do now as an old woman," Leah jokes, raising a sarcastic eyebrow.

Looking at this woman, who is so elegantly beautiful it's almost not fair, no one would dare think to call her old. I nod because I could use some advice and she had been in my shoes at one point.

"I used to look at love and being a couple as if it were falling into a fairy tale. You know when you see those kinds of people? The ones who seem like they're so in love that logic and reality don't touch them? I used to think that's how it was supposed to be. And then I met Killian. And he showed me that being with the person you're meant to be with doesn't have to be rainbows and unicorns. Life isn't like that, it's tough and gritty at times. You have losses, you get knocked down, and sometimes, you don't come out on top. Those people who see hearts and frolic in meadows? They're the ones who don't make it. You know who does? The tough couples, the ones who know how deep their feelings go but aren't blinded by them. The ones who don't get mired down in the illusion, those are the partners who make it.

The ones that can deal with meddling family members and crazy work schedules and sick children … that is the stuff that bonds you. Love is the bones, and those are necessary, but without wits … you've got nothing. Approaching life like that, with the person you chose above everyone else, is how you get through it. It's not about having thick skin, it's about being smart and logical, while also being in love."

Did this woman just invade my body and read every single thought and insecurity I have?

"Wow …" I breathe. "I think I might be in love with *you*."

Leah squeezes my arm, which is lying in the middle of our shared table. "You remind me of me when I first started dating Killian. And us WAGs, we've got to stick together. Especially the good ones like you, I want to see you soar. And girl, with a voice like that, you're going to knock 'em dead."

I'd come to Jude's game expecting a couple of hours of footie, and instead, I was given the greatest advice of my lifetime. My stroke of luck is infinite, these days.

40

JUDE

"To our boy, Jude! You always take a sad song and make it better!"

Kingston lifts his glass, giving a toast in my honor as everyone else clinks their drinks and then almost downs them.

"If I didn't love you like a brother, I'd wallop you for being so cheesy." I roll my eyes at him.

He loves to throw that Beatles song in my face every time I score a goal ... which I did tonight. And all with my best friend riding the bench and then being substituted in mid-match. That's right, Kingston is in London to stay, and signed his contract last night.

"But, I should add a toast for my main bloke, to his continued success." I hold up my glass, and the group of us toast Kingston.

In normal Kingston Phillips fashion, he climbs on top of the table, lifts his button-up shirt, and shows us all his abs. The group is comprised of a couple of our teammates, their wives or girlfriends, and then Kingston, Vance, Aria, and me. We decided on a late night dinner after the match at an old-school steak and seafood restaurant, and the smell of our appetizers alone reminds me I've been running about for ninety or so minutes.

"Get an eight-pack or stop boasting!" someone yells from across the restaurant.

Our heads turn, and Kingston's face sours as he sees the person heckling him from below. Poppy Raymond sits three tables over with a group of girls, and she's giving my friend the most bored expression I've ever seen.

"I do have an eight-pack, maybe you need your eyes checked. Better yet, come sit by me and I can check you out," Kingston lobs back.

"God, you're daft. It's a pity girls fall for those lines." Poppy rolls her eyes.

"And it's a shame that such a pretty package has such a bad attitude," he clips as he climbs down off the table.

"Oh, love, you wouldn't be complaining if you knew just how good it is under all this pretty packaging." Poppy smirks at him with a smile that could send any man to his knees.

"Can we please stop yelling across the restaurant?" Vance elbows Kingston in the gut.

Kingston lets out on *oomph* but stops shouting at Poppy. She turns back to her table guests, and he shoots daggers at her head for the rest of our meal.

"I got to sit with Leah Ramsey at the match," Aria tells me as her filet and my T-bone are set down in front of us.

Killian approached me on the sidelines during warm-ups, and I was glad to see him again. "That's nice, how was she? I've never formally met her, but isn't she like ... the American every British woman wishes to be?"

"Something like that. She's lovely, actually, and gave me some great advice."

"And what was that?" I say with my mouth full because I'm too hungry to care.

"That's for me to know, and you to reap the benefit of." Aria grins.

"Is it a sex thing? Because I'd be very grateful to her if it was a sex thing." I lower my voice so only my girl can hear me.

Aria rolls her big, beautiful eyes. "Is everything always about sex to you?"

"After I've run around a pitch for two hours, scored the victory goal, ate a nice, healthy portion of steak and now my girlfriend is sitting next to me in this dress that's riding up her thighs ... yes, it's all about sex."

I watch as her eyes melt into lustful pools of lava and use the opportunity to run a finger up her bare leg.

"You're rotten," she accuses me, but there is no malice in her tone.

If anything, she sounds two seconds away from begging me to take her home. It's a miracle I ever kept my hands off this woman for as long as I did in the beginning ... Aria is that irresistible to me.

"Good thing you're the one I get to spoil, then," I tease, pressing my lips to her neck.

Aria murmurs her agreement. "Good thing."

41

ARIA

"You sure you'll be okay for three days?" Doubt grips my stomach like a vice.

Dad waves at me and makes an annoyed cluck with his tongue. "Get out of here before I have to kick you out. I'll be fine. Mrs. Nethers from next door will check in on me every few hours, like a bloody babysitter. And I have all of my medications lined up."

"And meals prepped in containers in the refrigerator. Your transport for the doctor's visit is set up and will be here tomorrow at noon sharp. Don't stay up too late, and if you need anything, I'll have my cell phone on me."

He's on the last round of radiation after he completed chemo last week, but after the health scare he had, and the hospital, I am extremely hesitant to leave him.

"Would you scram already? You sound like the adult here, and that's not how it should be. You deserve a few nights off, love. Go have a brilliant time in Italy. I traveled to Positano once, the most beautiful place in the world ..."

Dad trails off, and I know he's leaving out the detail that he and my mother had gone there together. He talks about her so rarely, it's as if she'd never been in either of our lives at all. I was too young to fully grasp why she left, but if I had to guess from the heartbreakingly sympathetic looks Dad gave me whenever I'd asked as a child, I'd assume it was because she never really wanted to have children. My parents traveled the world before they had me in their late thirties, I remember looking at books filled with old pictures of their explorations.

Shaking my head, I resolve myself to stop letting the sadness of the past creep in and just create my own memories.

Jude and I only have a few days off before his international break is over, and my time in the studio starts. In a week, I'll go into twenty-hour sessions in the booth, working with producers and songwriters and music execs to pump out my album. Ian said they were hoping we could cut all the rough takes of the eight tracks in a month which means a lot of late nights and hard work. I'm not afraid of it, I've done backbreaking labor since I was in secondary school.

This is my passion, I'm not afraid of cutting my teeth to succeed at it.

Although, when I finally do emerge from the studio, it will be to help Dad through the recovery from his tumor removal. Dr. Bradley, his oncologist, is confident that in a couple of months, the tumor will be shrunken enough to operate, and Dad will be strong enough after laying off treatment for a while.

I am both terrified and elated for that time to come. On one hand, my father will finally be in remission after the surgery. He can have his life back, we can move, I can give him a new life where he can roam free of the house. But on the other, the operation isn't a guarantee, nor is the fact that the cancer will be completely gone. I try not to think about it too much, as I can't predict the future, or control it.

"I'll miss you. Send you postcards, okay?" I promise him as he wraps me in a hug.

"Postcards? I expect a lot more than that. I want good wine and pizza and beautiful leather goods," Dad jokes.

"I'll work on it," I tease back, but in all reality, I'll load bags full of those things if it will make him smile.

"Tell Jude to take care of my girl, okay?" he says into my hair, and I know it's a lot for him to trust another man with his daughter.

Speak of the devil, my gorgeous boyfriend slips through the front door, a witness to our goodbye.

"Ah, Jude, I was just talking about you. I told Aria you better take care of her, but now I can tell you face-to-face. I'm trusting you, and this is her first adult travel experience. No shenanigans, yeah?"

Jude nods solemnly. "None, sir. I'll have her home by curfew every night."

The scoundrel, he will not and we both know it. If anything, Jude is going to be the bad influence that makes me jump into the Italian ocean naked or some other ridiculous thing. I raise my eyebrow at him over my father's shoulder, and I know he's trying desperately not to crack a smirk.

"We should go, the plane isn't going to stay on the tarmac forever," Jude tells me.

A private plane ... who the bloody hell am I? I feel like my life has turned into one big romantic comedy, but since Jude is taking me to the Amalfi Coast, I'm not going to argue it. He convinced me, with his head between my thighs last night, that I deserve all the good that is finally coming my way.

Once we're in the car, with the driver directing us toward the airport, I finally let myself relax.

"What're you thinking about?" I ask Jude, settling in his long, lean arms.

How this man makes my heart and stomach both flip over simultaneously every time he touches me ... I'll never know.

"I keep thinking about how it'll be very difficult to stop myself from doing illegal things to you when I catch sight of your body in a bikini when we make it to the beach," he says very seriously.

That makes me bark out a crude laugh. "You're so bad."

"That's why you like me." Jude nuzzles my ear, tickling it a bit.

I shake my head, turning to look up at him. "No. That's why I love you."

EPILOGUE

ARIA

One Year Later

Glittering chandeliers cast light into every corner of the room, a golden hue coating everyone and everything I can see.

The party for my album release is more decadent than I thought it would be, and although it's been a bit since I stepped into this world, I'm still not fully comfortable in it.

I pull at the velvet fabric of my emerald dress, the one whose price tag I almost puked over when I saw it. This dress cost more than almost every item in my life put together. It's a rental for the night, something the stylist Barry hired told me, and so I keep fretting over getting any speck of food or drink on it.

"Relax, this is your night, and you look beautiful." Dad walks up, carrying a champagne flute in one hand and a mound of passed hors d'oeuvre in the other.

It's wonderful to see so much color back in his face. "Take it easy on the snacks, yeah? You still have a doctor's appointment next week."

"A little cheese and bacon isn't going to bring my cancer back, love." He kisses me on the cheek and walks off.

Even though he's in remission, I still worry constantly over him. It helps that we still live together, so I can check on him when I'm not traveling, working late nights, or staying with Jude in London.

I haven't allowed Jude to buy my father and I a flat in London, or more ridiculous, move us all into one of those beautiful white terrace houses in a posh neighborhood. However, I did enlisted his real estate prowess to help me purchase a moderately priced flat in Harlow with the advance I've been paid in anticipation of my album. An advance that, without Barry's help, wouldn't exist.

Jude and his management have helped me so much thus far, but I still have my independent spirit about me. I'm not going to let my rich and famous boyfriend pay my way, nor am I going to take advice from so-called professionals blindly. I examine every deal presented to me, I consult Dad on everything, and make a decision with my gut ... not market research or the pounds offered.

Which is how I produced an eight-track album, with my own original lyrics on every song, that I am fully proud of. I'd been stubborn in its creation, taking advice on the nose and doing the opposite. Ian was extremely frustrated at times, but I knew, at the end of it all, that I'd made an album that I was both excited by and could sell for the label. The fact that in two weeks, it would be played for the masses ... blimey, I still can't wrap my head around it.

The third song on *Hope*, the name of my album, pumps through the speakers that have been set up around the sparkling room. Industry professionals nod their head to the love ballad, while my friends and family keep throwing me thumbs-up every five seconds. It's a sip and listen kind of soiree, at least that's what Ian called it. And so far, he seems pleased with how the small crowd is receiving it.

Me? I am giddy as a schoolgirl that anyone is hearing my music. It's something I never in a million years thought would happen, and that's why I wanted to call the album Hope. This is the feeling I never dared to feel, and now I am putting it out into the world so others can have some if they need it.

Suddenly, an angry-faced hunk is heading straight across the room for me.

"You invited Poppy?" Kingston practically screams at me.

I shrug, a devious grin washing over my face. "We had a nice chat last time I saw her. I like her. Deal with it."

He points a finger at my face. "You're an inciting meddler."

I cackle. "That may be, but I'm dying to see the outcome of my troublemaking."

We all know that Kingston and Poppy will either kill each other, or fall madly in love ... which, of course, is why I invited her. I am part of a happy couple now, all I want is for others to feel the kind of affection I do. And if anyone can use some genuine care, it's Kingston Phillips. He might appear to have a fantastic ego and brutish snobbery, but underneath all of that is a man who is very much wounded from the mistreatment of his parents.

Now that Kingston and Jude have been promoted to the first team and are scoring goals like their jobs depend on it. Which, now that I say it, is kind of accurate ... they do have to perform to keep their positions. But it means that Vance is the only musketeer left at the academy. I can tell, each time he comes to London to stay with Jude, or we see him in Clavering, that he is retreating further into himself. I hope, for his sake, that something gives soon.

"Hey, so, I heard you're like, the second coming of Adele," a husky voice whispers in my ear.

I turn as Jude's arms wrap around my waist, the cocky grin of his beaming down upon me. "Hmm, I don't know about that. But I did hear that Jude Davies is at this party, think you could introduce me?"

"I thought you two were already *nicely* acquainted." Jude's naughty grin disappears as he kisses it into my own smiling lips.

Those sturdy, skilled hands sneak into the low dip of my dress, his fingertips skimming the flesh just above my tailbone. I get lost in the dance our mouths are doing until someone crudely interrupts us.

"Save it for the hotel suite after, lovebirds. I need you on stage." Barry practically pulls Jude away from me and waves a hand for me to follow him.

At the last minute, I lace my fingers through my boyfriend's. "I want you up there with me."

"It's your time to shine, love." Jude tries to extract his hand from mine.

"And without you, I wouldn't have any of it. So come on, before I make you."

His eyebrows raise. "I'd like to see how you can make me. Does it involve your mouth or your hands?"

Even now, a year and more after we first decided to be together, he can make me blush like mad. There are days we make each other mental, and days where I'm so caught up in him that I can't see anything else. The man that I love is arrogant and randy, but he's also loyal and kind and supports me more than anyone who has ever wandered through my life. There are no more doubts about what we are to each other, and I never have to second guess his feelings for me. I tame him just enough, and he lets me be wild.

He loves me, and I love him.

And together, we've taught the other what our life was missing.

F*ind out what happens between Kingston and Poppy, read The Lion Heart now!*

Read the rest of The Rogue Academy series, available now!

<u>The Second Coming</u>
<u>The Lion Heart</u>
<u>The Mighty Anchor</u>

ALSO BY CARRIE AARONS

Do you want your **FREE** Carrie Aarons eBook?

All you have to do is **sign up for my newsletter**, and you'll immediately receive your free book!

Then, check out all of my books, available in Kindle Unlimited!

Standalones:

If Only in My Dreams

Foes & Cons

Love at First Fight

Nerdy Little Secret

That's the Way I Loved You

Fool Me Twice

Hometown Heartless

The Tenth Girl

You're the One I Don't Want

Privileged

Elite

Red Card

Down We'll Come, Baby

As Long As You Hate Me

On Thin Ice

All the Frogs in Manhattan

Save the Date

Melt

When Stars Burn Out

Ghost in His Eyes

Kissed by Reality

The Prospect Street Series:

Then You Saw Me

The Callahan Family Series:

Warning Track

Stealing Home

Check Swing

Control Artist

Tagging Up

The Rogue Academy Series:

The Second Coming

The Lion Heart

The Mighty Anchor

The Nash Brothers Series:

Fleeting

Forgiven

Flutter

Falter

The Flipped Series:

Blind Landing

Grasping Air

The Captive Heart Duet:

Lost

Found

The Over the Fence Series:

Pitching to Win

Hitting to Win

Catching to Win

Box Sets:

The Nash Brothers Box Set

The Complete Captive Heart Duet

The Over the Fence Box Set

ABOUT THE AUTHOR

Author of romance novels such as Fool Me Twice and Love at First Fight, Carrie Aarons writes books that are just as swoon-worthy as they are sarcastic. A former journalist, she prefers the love stories of her imagination, and the athleisure dress code, much better.

When she isn't writing, Carrie is busy binging reality TV, having a love/hate relationship with cardio, and trying not to burn dinner. She lives in the suburbs of New Jersey with her husband, two children and ninety-pound rescue pup.

Please join her readers group, Carrie's Charmers, to get the latest on new books, exclusive excerpts and fun giveaways.

You can also find Carrie at these places:

Website

Amazon

Facebook

Instagram

TikTok

Goodreads

Made in the USA
Middletown, DE
29 October 2021